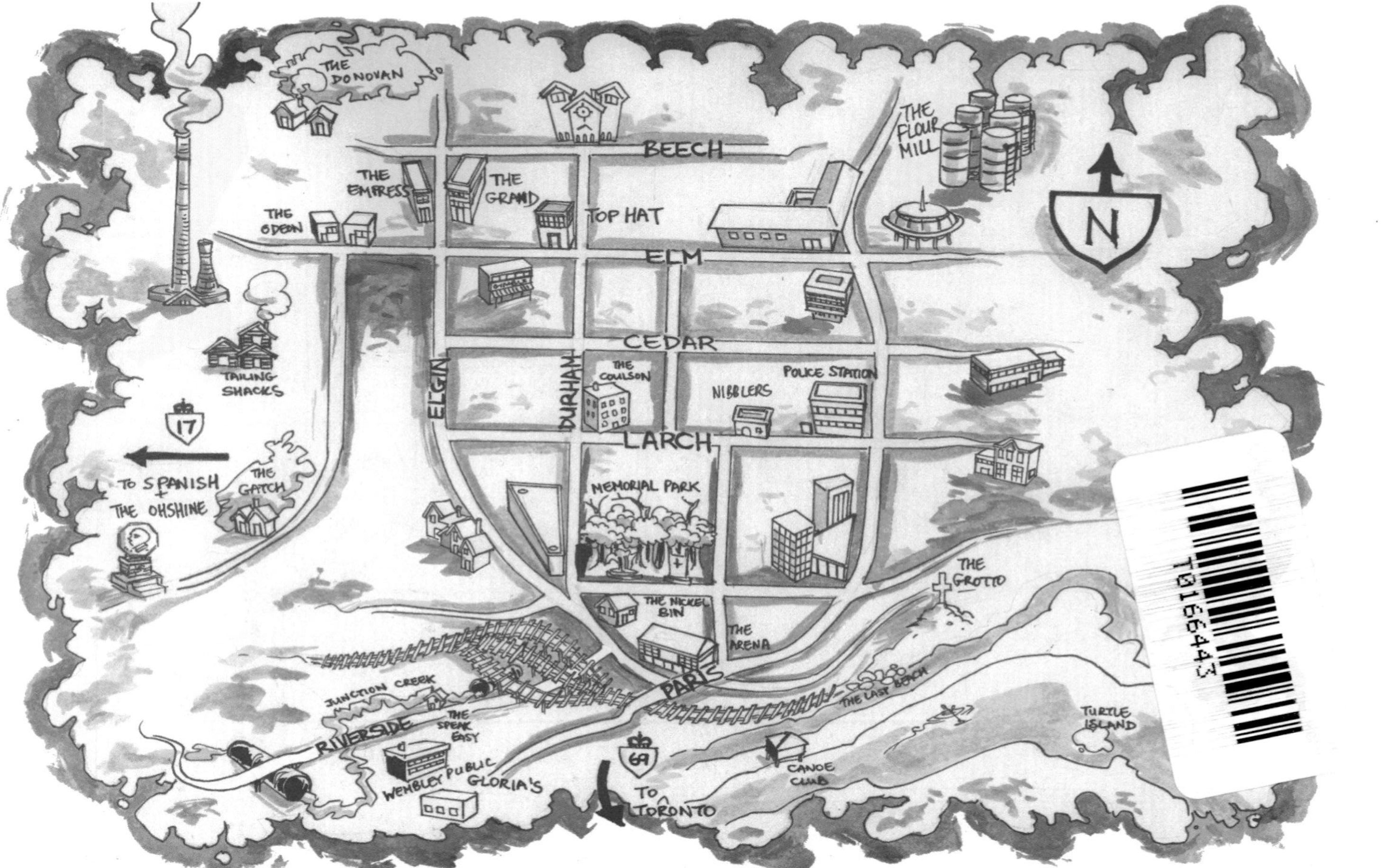

THE DONOVAN
THE FLOUR MILL
N
BEECH
THE EMPRESS
THE GRAND
THE ODEON
TOP HAT
ELM
CEDAR
ELGIN
DURHAM
THE COULSON
NIBBLERS
POLICE STATION
LARCH
TAILING SHACKS
17
TO SPANISH + THE OHSHINE
THE GATCH
MEMORIAL PARK
THE GROTTO
THE NICKEL BIN
THE ARENA
PARIS
JUNCTION CREEK
THE SPEAK EASY
RIVERSIDE
WEMBLEY PUBLIC
GLORIA'S
69
TO TORONTO
THE LAST BEACH
TURTLE ISLAND
CANOE CLUB

MATTHEW
HEITI

THE CITY STILL BREATHING

Coach House Books, Toronto

first edition

Canada Council for the Arts Conseil des Arts du Canada
ONTARIO ARTS COUNCIL CONSEIL DES ARTS DE L'ONTARIO
Canadä

Published with the generous assistance of the Canada Council for the Arts and the Ontario Arts Council. Coach House Books also acknowledges the support of the Government of Canada through the Canada Book Fund and the Government of Ontario through the Ontario Book Publishing Tax Credit.

LIBRARY AND ARCHIVES CANADA CATALOGUING IN PUBLICATION

Library and Archives Canada Cataloguing in Publication

Heiti, Matthew, 1980-, author
The city still breathing / Matthew Heiti.

Issued in print and electronic formats.
ISBN 978-1-55245-283-7 (pbk.).-- ISBN 978-1-77056-355-1 (epub)

I. Title.

PS8615.E377C58 2013 C813'.6 C2013-904091-9

The City Still Breathing is available as an ebook: ISBN 978 1 77056 355 1.

Purchase of the print version of this book entitles you to a free digital copy. To claim your ebook of this title, please email sales@chbooks.com with proof of purchase or visit chbooks.com/digital. (Coach House Books reserves the right to terminate the free digital download offer at any time.)

'Used to be, the invisible man was invincible in school.
But now.
He wanted to be a scientist and discover things.
A cure for cancer. New stars. New planets.
Somebody in Toronto already beat him to the discovery of penicillin.
And now.
Just sex and poetry.
And a taste for leaving.
Every time he walks down the street that leads out of town, his thumb breaks out in a rash.'

– Patrice Desbiens, *L'homme invisible / The Invisible Man*

'Here comes
Here comes another hard winter in Babylon
Where have you gone?
Damn you and the horse you rode in on
What star did you fall down from?
Why'd you have to be so cruel?
So cruel.'

– Kevin Quain, 'Winter in Babylon'

I

He just doesn't know what to do. Wally Kajganich standing on the side of the road shivering, wishing he hadn't stopped the van. It's been a cold day, the kind that punches you in the gut every time you step outside, and the coming night is promising worse. The water's turned to ice running down the rock, hanging in long fingers over the ditch. There's no snow on the ground yet, but that's not what makes the ice stand out – that's not what made Fisher call out or Wally hit the brakes. It's pink. Rosy explosions trapped beneath the layer of frost, racing down to the very tips of the icicles where the tint seems darker, more like some fancy lipstick red.

Nothing's been said for about five minutes, just two men standing on the gravel shoulder over the ditch, staring, and then Fisher opens his mouth once or twice before finally saying 'Well' without a question mark. Wally rubs his hands together, looks back at the transport van – police markings faded though he's put in two requests to have her repainted – and then walks farther down the shoulder, muttering 'Shit.' Fisher shuffling behind him like some lost puppy.

They find a point where the embankment is not so steep and the two men climb up the surface of rock and frozen moss, the exertion forcing clouds of vapour around their heads. They make their way back to the top of the ridge and do some more standing and staring.

'Hey, Kag, maybe it's this thing.'

Fisher's pointing at a little stone man perched on the lip of the embankment – the kind of thing you see up and down every highway and back road – making some kind of joke, which Wally knows because he's got that little twist to his lip he only gets when he makes lewd suggestions about women they drive by or female prisoners.

More sounds come out of Fisher, but Wally's got him on mute and is turned, looking back into the trees – evergreen and naked maples, thick and dark like a storybook. He's got that little tingle, that whisper behind his ear that used to make him think he could've been a good cop. Leads his eyes, tracing down the scarred trunks to the ground, telling him, *Look, look, it's right in front of you*. But all he can see is an ocean of cracked and browning leaves. *Look*.

A hand on his shoulder. 'C'mon. Celia's making me dinner.'

And it's just as he turns around that he spots it, the shock causing him to grab Fisher's hand, and the men stand, holding hands and staring down at an opening in the pile of leaves. An eye staring back up at them, frozen over like a marble.

By the time they get the leaves cleared away, Wally's hands are aching and he's got them locked over his mouth, blowing into them like a bellows – rhythmic wheezing in and out. Fisher looks at him and then down at the body and then back at him again.

'The hell you doin that for?'

He pulls his hands away, sliding them inside his jacket and under his armpits. 'My goddamn Raynaud's.'

Fisher steps back, wrinkling his nose. 'Your hand disease?'

'I'm not an effin leper.' Wally takes his hands out and blows into them, but Fisher's looking back down.

A cold wind rolls over the embankment – the brown hair lifts and waves in the wind and for a second the gesture's so easy you'd almost think he was just resting. But the skin's gone bone white, the lips frozen, curling back, and those eyes don't shut, and Wally wonders what kind of a man would lie naked on a rock or what kind of a man would put him there like that.

'Hell of a thing,' Fisher says for the fifth time, each time like it's just occurred to him.

Wally's only seen a body once before, seven years back now, two for the price of one. A car gone through the guardrails into a ravine out near Spanish. A yellow Beetle. You'd never expect to find such peace in the middle of all that mess, but death has a way of looking easy. Still, it gets stuck in your craw. Like this body, almost unmarked, glazed like some Italian sculpture he saw in a book once. But the throat opens in a smile, coal black along the slash. Blood frozen up the chin, following the jawline and then running along the ridge of the ear onto the rock, spilling down the slope, joining with a stream, finally freezing into a sheet of ice. Long bloody fingers.

'What d'you mean it's not working?'

'I mean it's not working.'

'It was working before.'

'Not working now.'

Wally tries the key again, but this time even the dashboard lights won't blink. Effin scrap metal. That's what they give him – won't paint her, won't service her. He wants to get angry, tries, but only some kind of numbness rises up from his belly. He stares out the window at all that asphalt in either direction. No one's passed them the entire time they've been here.

'Effin shortcut my ass.'

'Well, there's no traffic, is there?'

'Yeah and no help either.'

Stuck on this side road, still at least an hour west of the city. He can feel Fisher twitching, his big mouth winding up, but he gives him a look and grabs the radio. He cuts through the static and gets the dispatcher on, arguing with him about their unit number, reporting the body, explaining the dead battery, clarifying the battery and the body are two separate dead things, trying to give some idea of their location on whatever back road they happen to be stuck on. Back to static.

'What does he mean, "We'll get to you when we get to you"?'

'He means we're special constables driving an empty prisoner transport and they only give a shit about real cops.'

Fisher zips his jacket and pulls the hood up, arms crossed and sitting glumly. 'This is the wrong kind of special, Kag.'

It's just past five and the light's got that funny look when you know the bottom's about to drop out on the day. Wally balls up his fingers and toes, trying to urge some feeling into them. The temperature's still dropping in the cab of the van.

He swings the door open with a squeal of rusting metal.

Fisher bitches while Wally gathers wood, but when the pyramid is built, he wants to be the one to light it. Wally lets him grunt over the matches for a few minutes before taking over and getting the whole thing burning. He slowly gets some feeling back into his feet and hands, watching the chimney-red, pumpkin-orange flames, the little twist of blue playing in the throat of the fire. He pushes a big dead piece of maple in, lifting a cloud of sparks, lighting up the outline of the body a few feet away.

'Don't see why we gotta be so close to it,' Fisher says.

'So we can keep an eye on it, the van and the road.'

'Creeps me out.'

Wally looks across the fire at the younger man. Fisher's big arms wrapped around his legs, knees pulled up to his chin, his whisky-coloured face just barely visible, eyes darting nervously. Wally laughs, a single short bark. 'Didn't you come in from the Wiky reserve?'

'Yeah.'

'Shouldn't this be your natural element ... nature?'

Fisher's eyes swivel to Wally, twinkling, and he gets that twist to his mouth again. 'Christ, Kag, we live in houses now – you know that, right?'

The firelight catches the dark shapes of trees, dragging long shadows out of them – the forest leaning in, crowding next to them at the fire's edge. There is no wind, the only sound the popping of the wood.

'What d'you think – ?'

But Fisher leaves it like that, shaking it off with his head and burrowing down into his knees. Neither man has broken the heaviness to say much about it. To speculate about the why and how. Haven't used the words *him* or *body* or said anything about *dead* except on the radio. Something about the silence feels appropriate, or maybe it's an excuse to ignore the other feelings creeping in with the night.

Wally tries to imagine cutting Fisher's throat, watching him die, taking off all his clothes and leaving him here, on the rock above the road. It doesn't fit. He just can't conjure up that much hate for something. He tries to imagine coming out here, naked in the wilderness, and cutting his own throat, wanting to do that. It doesn't fit much better, but his stomach doesn't turn over at it.

'Maybe an animal done it.' Fisher's eyes on Wally again, something almost hopeful in the tone, like this might undo it, or make it more understandable.

Wally sees the fear coming in on his partner, the body making a space for itself next to the fire, and he clears his throat and starts the way the old-timers always started with him: 'Knew this one cop, working late, stalled out on a country road.' He gets into the one with the hook in the door handle and then the one about the knocking and the boyfriend hanging in the tree, and then the one about that Myllarinen kid who killed his own parents with a box cutter, true-story-I-swear, and at the end of it Fisher's fear returns to its normal ever-present level. They sit more easily around the fire, almost cozy, like camping if only they had some effin marshmallows.

'Ow!' Fisher grabs his cheek and looks around wildly. 'Something bit me.'

Another something hits the fire with a hiss. A pause and then the sky's vomiting pebbles of ice – fire sputtering, miniature explosions off the rocks and the metallic *ping ping* on the van below. Fisher jumps up and runs for cover, but Wally's yelling brings him back.

'Take the feet.'

He's already got his hands under the armpits – the feeling of the flesh, cold and hard, coming through his gloves. Fisher's looking at him and the body like he's gone nuts, shouting over the rushing sound of the hail all around them.

'Where are – ?'

'Take the feet!'

Wally starts to drag the body, but Fisher grabs it around the ankles, lifting the stiff thing between them. They struggle down the embankment, hailstones cracking off the body, ripping small pockets in the frozen skin. Wally, unseeing through the downpour, bangs into the back of the van, stumbling and losing hold of his end. The head hits the gravel, bending the neck forward at an unnatural angle, the gashed throat yawning open toward Fisher, who lets go of the whole thing.

Wally swings the rear doors open, but Fisher can only stare down at the body. He's not saying anything but Wally knows he's asking why. Why why why.

Fisher peers through the slot into the back of the van. 'Celia's not gonna be happy with me working at no Deluxe Fries.'

'It'll be fine, Fish.'

'It's in the handbook. You don't fuck with a … a crime scene.'

'You rather we leave it out there – get all torn up or some animal make off with it?'

'No … just rather keep my job, is all. Rather we didn't have him back there. Guess he's better than some of the shit chuckers we drive around with.'

Wally slides the slot door closed. 'It's not a him anymore.'

The two men are sitting in the cab, wrapped in the coarse wool of the emergency blankets, breath already frosting over the windows. The gunfire rattle of hailstones has slowed. It's quiet, almost peaceful. Wally feels his eyes shut.

Then out of nowhere – a woman singing. He opens his eyes and sees Fisher fiddling with the tape deck.

'What the eff is that?'

'It's my Crystal Gayle.'

'Fish!' Wally slams the eject button. 'We might need the last of the battery for the radio.'

'Oh.' Fisher wipes his nose and rolls the snot nervously between his thumb and pointer finger. 'We gonna freeze to death in here, Kag?'

Wally takes in his partner, sees the joke but feels the concern underneath it. 'They say if you wanna make it through a cold night up north, best thing is to hunker down in a bag naked with someone else.'

Fisher looks at him with a big grin that moves back some of the worry he's been sucking on. 'Love to see them find us all here in the morning – three buck-naked men in a van.' He puts his chair back, reclining, scratching his smooth chin with a bare hand before shoving it back in the mitt. 'Drive em, drop em off and drive back, but goddammit, Kag, if you didn't have to stop on the coldest day of the year. Just you getting cold feet, I guess.'

'What the hell about?'

'Your date.' Fisher giggles like they're thirteen years old.

'I don't have a date. It's just lunch. Anyway, you were the one hollerin.'

'Cold feet is why you stopped, is alls I'm saying.' Fisher sighs and the joke's gone. 'Be eating dessert right about now, I guess. Celia's apple pie, apples off her dad's farm, still warm. She probably did a fresh loaf of bannock too – never ate the shit growing up, but she makes it so thick and flaky, it just melts. The side, she's got some carrots with butter and a bit of honey … '

Wally listens to Fisher working his way backwards through this meal, sharing each dish, the smells and textures, his voice becoming thicker with every slice of rare steak, mouthful of garlicked potatoes, murmuring into the easy ritual of setting the table, the hiss of a beer cap coming loose. Opening the front door, the warm rush of air as you cross from the rest of the world into your own little piece of it.

When Fisher moves off to sleep, Wally breathes on the window, drawing a circle with his glove and rubbing a porthole through the frost. He's hoping for the moon, a few stars, just a bit of light so he can know which way this van is pointing. But he can't see anything. Only this great hungry darkness.

He thinks about the body in the back and tries to make a story for this man. Thinks about the lonely kind of life you'd have to live for this lonely kind of end to it. A plain face, no identifying marks on the body, no identification of any kind, nothing to call his own. Probably middle-aged, halfway into some kind of life, some kind of career. Nothing really fulfilling. A failed relationshop, the usual wreckage. No kids. Colleagues, people to shoot the shit with – talk about the hockey game – but no real friends. Drinks too much. Watches too much television. Spends too many evenings alone. No devastating failures but no real sense of accomplishment. Had some potential at one time, now no real value. No real loss.

He pulls off his gloves, blowing into the bowl of his hands. As he pulls away to rub them, he sees his fingers already going yellow-white with the cold and then the shine of the ring he probably shouldn't be wearing anymore.

A wind is kicking up outside, gently rocking the van like a cradle.

Wally wakes because the feeling's gone out of his hands and feet. His fingers feel thick as he pulls them out of the gloves, jams them under his armpits and holds them there. Then he takes off his boots and socks and rubs at his feet, unsettled by the feeling of not feeling when his numb fingers touch his numb toes. Nothing he's doing brings the sensation back. He looks over at Fisher, head rolled on his shoulder and a line of drool down to his chin.

There's the creak of metal from the back, and Wally turns his head to the slot to listen. A sudden cold gust, like an exhalation, seems to leak in around the seams of the slot and he wonders if one of the rear doors has been left open.

He reaches out and fumbles with stiff fingers at the slot, finally getting the catch and sliding the door open to see two marbled eyes pressed up against the opening, staring at him. A second exhalation from the other side and Wally is hit by a coldness he's never known.

He slides the door closed again.

He falls back into his seat, his breath coming out in a cloud, already disbelieving. He wants to open the slot, to prove it's just his twisted imagination, but he is paralyzed by what he might find instead. The numbness crawls from his fingers and toes inward, turning his legs and arms to stumps.

It takes minutes or hours, but the cold seeps deeper into him, silencing each organ, stopping his blood, shrivelling his penis, slowly turning his body into a great weight. His head is being dragged down by this weight, to stare at this pale, useless thing attached to it. He knows the flesh is dying, but all he can feel is this great fatigue at the long road being put behind him. No real value. No real loss.

Lights and colours reel around him, igniting this useless body, and when he finally hears a knock at his window, Wally finds he can move again.

The cavalry is an asshole named Simpson who makes a lot of noise about taking their badges and dumping them back on the side of the road before he finally gives them the boost they need and tells them to take the corpse in anyway. There's light coming over the hills as they take off down the road to swing onto Highway 17 and head back east into the city. Fisher's been driving and talking a mile about his big plans for the future: '... I get back I'm gonna put in for the big time – provincial, city, don't give a damn. No offence, Kag, driving with you is fine, but I'm just done with all this shit. Don't know how you put up with it so many years.'

Wally nods and checks the speedometer. Fisher's all amped up and driving too fast as usual, but this time he doesn't say anything about it, turning to the window instead. He puts his hand on the glass, thinking through this sensation, the cool surface against his palm. Outside, a light snow has begun to fall, settling on tree branches and dusting the highway.

'They don't hurry up, not gonna find out anything about this guy's story.' Fisher adjusts the mirror and brushes at his hair. 'The first snow covers everything.'

Wally slides the slot door open and looks into the back. The hold has a padded bench on each wall and a bucket under one of these benches for emergencies. The first rays of sunlight are coming in at an angle through the rear windows, splashing across the floor. He notices he's been holding his breath only when he sees the body laid out, a thin vapour rising as it thaws.

He turns back to the window, watching for the big coin monument on the hill to let him know they're home.

2

Normando sits on the tail of his Warlock, bow legs dangling, sun coming up. He uses the fender of the truck to pop the cap on his Northern and takes a long pull of warm beer. Scratches his belly through blue-checkered flannel, looks at the twenty-foot head of King George looking back at him. Damned big thing. Bunch of damned wood with some silver paint – doesn't know that but it's what he's heard.

A red two-door pulls up, kicking gravel. Laughter and teenagers sliding out. The girl skips up to the pedestal, suddenly self-conscious as she poses underneath the damned big thing while the boy Polaroids her. She's in her pyjamas, for chrissakes. Normando slips off the tailgate, knees cracking, and limps to the edge of the hillside, the town spilling out before him. His back hurting like it always does, only worse.

He breathes it in, the fall air and dead-looking trees on the neighbourhood lanes, the black rock hills jumping up, leaning over the houses clustered around and beneath them. He has gone up and down every one of those streets. This is his town.

The long keen of a whistle and an old itch tells him the morning shift's going underground. He turns back to King George, the face on the giant coin glowing in the early sun. At its base, those two damned kids rolling around on the ground like it's *their* town. Like there could never be nothing else around that alive.

Behind them he catches the black smoke coming off the smelter. Getting on fine without him.

3

Francie Duluoz opens her eyes and sees the mobile above her bed going lazy one way and then back, just like it's been doing every morning since her dad put it up there when she was three. The light through the shutters on the carpet, the poster of Ivan Doroschuk on her door, the stairs, one two three fourteen of them, the kitchen with the butterfly wallpaper, her favourite bowl, favourite spoon, the taste of the cereal so known, so familiar that it's no taste at all. Moving through everything this morning just like yesterday and the day before and every day of Francie's days on this planet to now.

She sucks up the last of the milk in her bowl and fiddles with a pad and paper on the kitchen table. She gets as far as *dear mom and dad* before running out of words. There's the purring of a car over gravel and she scratches out the *dear*, heads for the back door. Grabs her bag on the way.

The Duluoz backyard is a dead, overgrown mess. Even in summer, but now in the late fall, it's greyer and deader than ever. Her dad pays attention to the front because that's what the neighbours see. The back is his own damn business. Let her mom plant tomatoes or something. But there're so many roots the only thing that grows is rhubarb. Francie hates rhubarb, and strawberries and pie crust by association.

Slim's on a branch of the old twisted maple. Wearing that smelly denim jacket with the sleeves too short. Trying to look like a rebel and maybe he does a bit. Right away she sees him dangling his new fashion statement from the branch. Cowboy boots.

'Where'd you get those shitkickers?'

'Found em. Around.'

She sits on the ground, back against the trunk. 'Liar.'

He laughs because they both know it's true. Slim always lying about everything because he thinks it's funny. Because it's easier that way. He pulls a sucker out of his pocket, peels the plastic and tosses it in the breeze.

'That's littering, y'know.'

He shrugs, sticks the sucker in his mouth. 'When're your parents back?'

'Funeral's today, so probably tomorrow.' Feeling with her hand the place he cut their initials in the bark. 'You're late.'

'It's early.'

'You're still late.'

He drops out of the tree and heads for the driveway. 'Let's book then.'

'I'm in my fuckin pyjamas, Slim.'

'They look great.'

Francie grabs her bag and follows him out to the red Dart, all polished up and not a spot of rust on her. On the passenger side, Slim runs his hand from headlight to handle, touching it like he touches Francie sometimes when nobody would notice. He swings the big door open for her. She tries to duck past him, but he grabs her bag.

'Trunk's full.' He tosses it in the back seat. 'That all you got?'

'Don't need much.' She looks up at the house. Grey with burgundy trim – like Cape Cod, her dad said, like this was cultured, like this was the excuse for never repainting and letting it peel like some old onion. The house of yesterday and the days and days before, the house of this morning, and that was it.

Slim clicks the heels of the cowboy boots together three times and holds the door wide for her. 'No place like home.'

As they pull away, she watches her upstairs window, catching a bit of her mobile. Spinning one way and then back.

Francie rolls down the window to let in the fall air and when Slim gives her The Look she says, 'It stinks,' because it does. Slim cleans the dash with a toothbrush and vacuums the upholstery, but the car still reeks three years after Heck puked in the back. Four milkshakes and an hour swinging around in a rubber tire and no amount of shampoo can get the smell out. Today worse than usual.

Slim crosses Regent and trucks on down Ontario, hardly a car out yet. 'Where're we going?'

'Got a couple stops to make.' He rubs his eyes, red rimmed and grey bagged. Scratches some of his poor excuse for stubble.

'You look tired.'

'What?' He puts a hand on her leg like he's trying to reassure her. But the hand is a dead thing weighed down by that big dumb gold watch and he's looking at the road with some thousand-mile stare like he's seeing anything but her, this car, this road.

'You okay, Slim?'

He takes his hand away and pops in the New Order eight-track, Francie's favourite. The same album they played racing through the slag heaps in summer, sweating and tangled in Slim's secret cabin, talking their way into the next day, the next month, all the nexts you could come up with. Music sounds different on different days. Today as that echoing guitar kicks in, all she can hear is the grey blue of all the loneliness in the world. Both of them singing along, *I've lost you, I've lost you, oh, I've lost you.* Slim slapping the steering wheel out of time as the drum rolls on.

He pulls right up to the base of it and pops the parking brake on. Francie staring up at the big coin. 'You're kidding, right?'

Slim reaches across her to the glove compartment and pulls out his Polaroid. Swings his door open. 'C'mon.'

'You're not kidding.'

'People get their picture taken with the Eiffel Tower, don't they?'

'It's so tacky.'

'We'll do a whole series of you in front of giant coins. Big dimes, big pennies. It'll be my first show.'

He laughs, Slim all over again, and his laugh is so stupid, honking like a goose, that she's laughing too. Out of the car, him chasing, her dodging. She jumps up on the concrete base and strikes a pose, something she saw in a magazine, one leg bent and a hand on her cheek. Slim goes down on one knee, holding the camera like a rifle, a real professional.

'Hey, isn't that Normando?' Slim points his camera off to the side and buzzes a Polaroid through.

She follows his aim and sees they're not alone – off at the end of the lot, a black truck, some ugly old man sitting on the fender staring at her with ugly eyes, drinking an ugly beer. 'Who?'

'The popcorn guy. Y'know, with the popcorn cart?'

'The one who eats children?'

'He doesn't eat – Jesus, he's like a local legend, Francie. They practically built the city around him.'

He looks like he could be that old. All the ugly oldness of this city. She'd been to Toronto last summer. Those high-rise apartments up in the clouds. All the restaurants and shops. Everything so new and fun and everything even uglier when she got back here.

The buzz of the Polaroid brings her back to Slim, grinning up at her.

'Catch me!' And she's jumping off the pedestal, Slim trying to grab her with one arm, protecting the camera, both of them tumbling over in a dusty laughing heap. She looks up at the big dumb coin. Laughing at this great tourist act. Laughing that in all the days of Francie's days on this planet, this is her first time up here. The whole city down there and the rim of slag like a ring tight around the two of them. She laughs so hard she might puke. 'Oh god I hate this place.'

She dozes off in the car for what feels like five minutes and then they're stopping already. Slim pulling up at Gloria's and she says, 'It'll be midnight before we get there.'

'I'm hungry.'

She sighs, making it as noisy as possible and says, 'I'll meet you inside' in a wait-for-me way. But he's already out and slamming the door. She pulls the rear-view down and checks her hair, ties it up to one side. She thinks about changing out of her pyjamas but doesn't.

Every girl in her graduating class wore a pound of makeup. Her friend Caitlin says she's a natural beauty, but that's just another way of saying princess and she isn't that. She just doesn't like makeup and anyway she does wear a bit of eyeliner now and then. If she feels like it. But not now, now she looks like she just crawled out of bed, but Slim says she looks good any time of the day. The way he takes her picture, he has a way of making her feel easy – not in *that* way – but in that moment, in the camera flash, she feels like she can be whatever it is she's gonna be.

Whatever. She gets out of the car. Slim's waited just long enough to start to wonder.

It's a blue haze inside the diner, graveyard shifters and nine-to-fivers rubbing elbows over greasy plates and bad coffee. Francie finds Slim in the corner booth, leg up, showing off one of the new boots, back to the wall, reading the menu like it's the work of one of his Russian poets. Two steaming mugs on the table.

Here comes Lucy, her shoulders all hunched up in her ears, gum going. 'What can I get you?'

'I'm fine with coffee.' Francie slides the menu across the table and Lucy snatches it away, swivelling her little eyes onto Slim.

'Two eggs over hard, home fries, brown toast.'

'Only got white.' Scribbling on her notepad like she might need to testify later. 'Ham, bacon, sausage.'

'Nope.'

'Eh?'

'No meat.'

'It comes with meat.'

'I don't want it.'

'No meat?' Like she's never heard of this before, like he might as well eat a baby as eat breakfast without meat.

'Nope.'

She gives him a nuclear stare and then walks off to the kitchen, still shaking her head as the doors swing closed.

Francie goes through her pockets and comes out with her pack of smokes, lights one. Slim giving her That Look. 'What? It's a menthol.' He shrugs as if he doesn't care and looks away. 'So I'm thinking, first thing we do is we start looking for an apartment.'

'Thought your sister had space.'

'She does, it's just my parents are going to *kill* her when they find out. And we can find something closer to school so you don't have to drag all your lenses and stuff around on the subway.'

'You know how expensive rent is, Francie?'

'I know.' The diner coffee is brewed so black she might glow in the dark. Slim not even touching his. Habits are reassuring. Something to collect, like she used to do with her marbles. Handfuls of alleys and a few croakers still in a bag in her closet. Left behind. 'But I'll get a job or something for a bit and I'll be pulling in some money soons I get an agent.'

'Right. Might as well get a penthouse, all the cash from the magazine covers.'

'Don't.' That easy, with a tone or a word or a look, to take all the light out of it. To puncture a dream. Like Francie's sister using a pin on a balloon at her birthday party and her crying, Dad coming over with more, no one understanding that other balloons were not *that* balloon. So easy to make someone else feel stupid. 'Don't make fun of me.'

'Sorry.' Because he sees right away what he's done, and all of a sudden he lets himself not be cool. The leg comes down and he leans across, takes her hand. 'You're fucking gorgeous.'

'Sure sure.'

'You are. To the max. You'll be all over the place – billboards, TV.'

'It's not about that, it's just … I want it so bad. I'll work my ass off.'

'You'll be fine. You're gonna be great. '

'And you'll do the photo shoots. My personal photographer.'

'Sure.' His hand's still there but now he's pulling away.

'When you can. You'll be busy with school and putting on art shows at little museums. I'll help you hang the photos. I'm good at that.'

He leans back to make room for the plate Lucy drops in front of him. Heaps of everything, bacon piled on the side, oozing grease. She refills Francie's mug. 'No school today?'

Slim answers by driving his bacon onto the tabletop with his fork. Lucy almost chokes on her gum. 'Slim Novak, you little devil.'

'It's Slider. My last name is Slider.'

'What?' Lucy's eyes bug out like a cartoon character and Francie swallows a giggle.

'Yeah, I changed it.'

'Your poor mother,' Lucy says with a huff and then she's off with her coffee pot, spreading joy.

Slim picks at his potatoes. Francie grabs a piece of his toast, too bleached for him to eat. 'If we leave right after this, we'll be there by one, right?'

'Mm.'

'I can't wait to get there. We can go get some food at this rad little Mexican place around the corner from Morgan's – you'll love it.'

'Mm.'

He's not looking at her, but she doesn't need his eyes to see right into him. Some people say that whole eyes-are-the-window thing, but with Slim it's his forehead. Which eyebrow is up, how many creases, one two or three, what shade of red is streaking across – an equation only she understands. Not just a window but an airplane hangar into his soul. 'You're not comin, are you?'

'What?' Dropping his fork. 'What are you talking about – I told you we were going. We're going.'

'You're acting all weird – what's your damage?'

'I'm tired.'

'That's not it.'

Big sigh. *Francie you're such a child.* 'I had to pawn some stuff, okay?'

'What stuff?'

'The lens pack, my flash ... the Nikon.'

'Your gear?'

'Yeah.'

'But you loved that camera.'

'Yeah, well I pawned it at Oz's.'

'Why the hell?' She can feel her voice rising and she catches Lucy giving them a nasty look from a table over.

'For money – that's why you pawn stuff, Francie.'

'But we got enough for the trip.'

'Yeah, for the trip, but that's not enough.' He's been playing with the salt shaker, wiggling it like a little man across the tabletop, like this conversation isn't worth anything. But she grabs his hand and the touch brings his eyes up.

'Why didn't you pawn your stupid watch then?'

He pulls his hand away and picks at that chintzy gold thing around his wrist. 'It was my dad's, Francie.'

'It's not even real.'

'Francie.'

A dumb thing to say, even she knows it. 'We gotta get your gear back – we'll just return the money.'

'Fuck it. Listen, Francie – ' He reaches into his jacket pocket and comes out with a crumpled envelope, and his eyes are no window, but she can see he's going to say something real and true for the first time in forever. But then he looks past her and the envelope disappears back into a pocket.

'Hey hey hey!' This moment broken by Heck sliding into the booth next to her, already munching away on a slice of bacon he's grabbed from the tabletop. 'So today's the big day or what?'

'Where the hell'd you come from?'

Heck pulls at his long hair with bacon-fatted hands, making sure it's smooth down his shoulders, then picks at his bangs. 'Mom dropped me off.' He takes a sip from Francie's mug, looks at her over the edge. 'Jeepers, why're you still wearing your jammies?'

Francie pulls her mug away, the handle all coated with grease. 'How'd you know we were here?'

'Slim called me.' Something bangs under the table and Heck grabs his knee. 'Ow, fuck, I mean I saw Slim's car. What the hell'd you kick me with – steel toes?'

Slim flashes his new boots.

'Where'd you get those?'

'Yeah, where'd you get those, Slim?'

'Kicked some guy's ass last night and took em.'

'Whoa! Didja?'

'Liar,' Francie says.

'Didja, Slim?'

Slim just leans back and smiles all mysteriously.

'Didja go all Macho Man on him?' Heck starts thrashing around, flexing his biceps. 'Like, ooh yeah!'

'Shut up, Heck.'

'Flying elbow drop!'

'Heck.' Francie cutting in. 'What're you doin here anyway?'

'Well, I just wanted to say goodbye. Or whatever ... ' He trails off, giving a look around like he's making sure no one's listening, then coming back to Slim. 'So where is it?'

'Shut up, Heck.'

'Where's what?'

'Oh shit, you didn't tell – '

'Shut up, Heck.'

'Tell me what?'

'Oops.'

'Nothing.'

'Yeah, nothing.'

'Sounds like something.'

'No it's nothing. Totally nothing. We're not talking about anything.'

'Shut up, Heck.'

Then there's silence and sitting, Slim looking out the window, Heck at the floor and Francie at everyone, trying to figure out what she should be getting ready to be angry about. Slim sucks his teeth and slides out of the booth. 'Let's book.'

Heck stuffs the last of the bacon in his mouth, a piece of toast, one more sip of coffee, and then he's out the door after Slim. Francie stuck with the bill.

She focuses on the window – the grey bungalows and grey sky and a few grey snowflakes snaking the grey pavement and grey morning oozing into grey afternoon – everything a grey paste moving by, helping her block out all that silence coming from Slim. Heck chattering away in the back seat, something about a movie he saw at the Odeon, like anyone gives a shit.

All that grey it's a wonder the city doesn't just puke it all up. A big wave right down Highway 69, the Dart riding the front of it all the way to Toronto. All of it giving over to the colour of Yonge Street, the spinning neon of Sam the Record Man, the grey in her sucked out just like that. But instead Slim has them going against it, right back into the ruined heart of the city, back downtown. She cracks her window, lights a menthol and lets the smoke trail out with all the rest of it.

When Slim parks at the end of Durham, she lets him ask twice, 'You coming?' Her still staring out the window, not saying boo. In the reflection, Slim's forehead set like when his mom talks to him, and she knows she could bitch at him from now until Christmas but it'd just be a waste of good bitching. She lets him get out without asking a third time because her silence is the only weapon she's got against all that forehead.

Heck halfway out the back seat, head flicking between Slim going and Francie staying. 'You guys.' He laughs, one forced note he swallows before it's done. He plays with the zipper on his ski vest, ahems a few times and then, 'You got any quarters? I gotta play some Rygar.'

'What's goin on, Heck?'

'What? With what? Nothin.'

She angles the rear-view so she can see his face. 'What's up with him?'

He squirms around in the back seat. 'I'll just get some quarters inside.'

After he's gone she looks back out the window, Christ the King down at the end of the street, a bit of pale sun coming through, lighting up the big stained-glass rose window in the tower. The first colour she's seen all day.

She changes in the back seat, jeans and her favourite purple Vuarnet sweatshirt, and she's still trying to dig the underwear out of her ass when she gets to the sign, that big monkey grinning down on all the traffic passing by. Top Hat Amusements.

Inside it's all lights and noise – pinball machines and pool tables and arcades and all the other shit she grew out of ages ago. Kids in outfits so lame it'd make you sick, things they were wearing down south like last year. Kids skipping class to go to the arcade, while their parents skip work to go to Elm Town Square or Towers or god knows where, just to get away from something. Each other maybe.

Francie makes for the back where the old ones hang out, past Heck shouting, 'Fuck, fuck, fuck,' at some cabinet, passing Feldman leaning against a pillar keeping an eye out, and there's Slim lounging at the Moon Patrol tabletop, across from Duncan, who's plucking at his green mohawk. They're just finishing up, Dunc sliding a small vial across and Slim sliding a few bills back.

Before Slim spots her, she ducks into the photo booth, sits on the ripped leather cushion in all that beaver panel. Her fingers find the cool disc of a quarter in her pocket and she thinks, like what the fuck, and drops it down the slot. The machine purrs and then Francie hears Slim's chair slide back and then Dunc's raspy voice.

'Slim, thought you should know – Milly's comin in from Spanish.'

'Okay.'

'He's looking for his brother.'

'Okay, so?'

'Disappeared a few days ago, just walked straight off the farm, and y'know Lemmy's a fuckin retard, so Milly figures he mighta got himself froze to death.'

'Bummer.'

'Yeah, so anyway, word is cops found some dead kid out on 17 last night.'

'Lemmy?'

'Dunno, but Milly thinks maybe, so he's comin to make sure. He fuckin loves that kid, practically raised him.'

'That's a bummer.'

'Yeah. Anyway, I'm just sayin cause the word is the cops lost the body.'

A shutter click, a flash, and Francie's world is a white sheet.

'So maybe someone took it or somethin. That's what's goin around anyway – that someone took it.'

Click, flash.

A groan from Slim. 'Fuckin Heck.'

Click, flash.

'Yeah, well, anyway, thought you should know. It's gonna look pretty bad for whoever stole that body. Milly sure loved that kid.'

Click, flash. She rubs her eyes. Trying to brush the white spots out.

A clunk and a strip spits out of the machine. Slim walks past the booth, heading back into the mass of brats. Francie grabs the strip, four white squares fading in, and stuffs it into her pocket, slides out of the booth. Dunc leaning over the tabletop, his face lit up by the game like he's telling a ghost story and maybe he is. He flashes her some teeth. 'Hey, Fran*cine*.'

She gives him the finger and heads for the door, dragging Heck away from his game yelling, 'Fuck, fuck, fuck,' the whole way.

Back in the car she doesn't bother with the window anymore, she stares straight at Slim. Even Heck shuts up when he feels the air go sour, or he's still sulking about his stupid arcade game. Slim keeps giving her sideways glances and his forehead's softened up. Then they turn off Regent and she finally loses it.

'Where the fuck are we going?'

'Just hold on.'

'I'm not gonna fuckin hold on. We're supposed to be halfway to Toronto but instead we been driving all over the city and I wanna know what the fuck for!'

'Just one last stop, Francie.'

'I swear to god, Slim, if we're not on that highway – I swear to fuckin god.'

'I'll get you there, don't worry, babe.' And it's got to be real bad, because pet names make Slim barf. As some kind of peace offering, he jams the tape back in the eight-track. The vocals kicking in, and *I'm stuck here two years too long*, and Francie thinks ain't that the fuckin truth of it. In the summer this was a love song and now it's a song about this day and yesterday and all the days before. Stuck, stuck, stuck. And then Bernard's voice gets all crunched up as the deck mangles the tape. Francie wrenching it loose.

'You're gonna wreck it, Francie!' Slim trying to grab the tape from her, but she rolls down her window and tosses it. 'Fuckin psycho!' He pounds the wheel.

Heck forces one of his stupid pig laughs from the back seat. 'You guys.'

In the mirror, she watches the magnetic tape unspooling behind them in a big oily ribbon, the tape clattering on the pavement. Francie laughing. Just Married.

Slim swings the car around behind Wembley Public, stopping in the trees down near the metal bridge over the creek. So far past talking, the three of them just watch the water, a shopping cart upended in the middle, brown foam pooling around it.

Slim pulls the vial out of his jacket and spills three blue microdots into his hand. He drops one and passes one back to Heck. The last one to Francie, her holding the blue tab like a bug she might squish. Placing it on her tongue. Dropping this little bit of colour down her throat, down inside her. A little blue into all that grey, like the food colouring her mom used for cake icing. Sometimes a little drop is all it takes. The blue's falling into her and outside the snow is just starting to fall.

Before five minutes have passed, Heck's already rubbing his face. 'It stinks back here.'

Slim snorts. 'Because you fuckin blew chunks back there.'

'It really stinks.' Heck's struggling out of his jacket. 'And it's hot, like a sauna.' Then he's out the door, rolling around on the gravel.

Francie pulls her legs up on the seat, chin on knees. 'I don't wanna be dicked around, Slim.'

'I'm not dicking you around.'

'You're lying – '

'I'm not – '

' – or you're not telling me something, whatever, I don't even give a shit, I just want to get down south.'

'What's the big deal? Toronto's nothin special.'

'It's better than here. There's so much to *do* there.'

'There's stuff here too.'

'Like what – hanging out at the arcade? What's up with you, I thought you hated it here too.'

He shrugs. 'It's okay.'

'It's not okay – it sucks! I want to do things, I want to be something, and this town is dead. It's dead. You can't be a photographer here.'

'Who says I can be a photographer anywhere?'

'Your stuff is so cool, Slim. The way you take people – it's so fuckin cool. Nobody's cool like that.'

'It's kids' stuff. I'm done with it.'

'Why're you saying that?' The blue is spreading through her, syruping over the grey, tinting everything. 'You don't mean it.'

'Photography – art, whatever – it's not *real*, Francie.'

'But what about school?'

'Fuck it.'

'You said it's one of the best in the country.'

'Well, I was wrong. It's stupid. I'll get a real job.'

'Where?'

'Wherever. Maybe you should think about it too.'

'I don't wanna be a fuckin waitress, Slim.'

'My mom's a waitress.'

'Yeah and you hate her.'

'I'm just saying maybe it's time you gave up this fantasy, Francie.'

'Shut up.' Flakes of blue coming down, everywhere they hit, the grey going blue, the ground the trees the hood of the car, a world of blue. 'Just tell me.' But Slim's face goes even greyer, becomes an iceberg. 'Are we going or not?'

And he opens his mouth, so wide his skull might crack, and out comes the grey of the word *No*, all that grey spilling across his seat toward her and she swings the door open, falling back onto the dirt on her ass, the world rolling underneath her like dad's sailboat on the lake in the summer, stumbling across the deck, scattering stones down into the water, her a stone, Slim's words scattering her, sending her forward over the edge of the boat, and she's falling down down down into the lake the creek the water down into Slim's mouth she's drowning in all that grey drowning in the pit of this town today tomorrow next all the nexts of Francie's days on this planet, one grey mess, and then she catches herself. Her hands on the railing. The cold of the metal. Something solid under her feet. The bridge. The creek below her.

Her hands around the railing blue. The bridge blue. Her insides the blue world. She's colder than she's ever been, so far beyond cold she misses the plain numb of grey.

Something slides around her, someone holding her – no, a jacket – Slim's jean jacket around her, the warmth of his body whispering around inside, but even this warmth just another kind of cold. She pulls it tight around her anyway.

'Dear Mr. Slider.' Slim leaning on the railing beside her. He's got that envelope from the diner and a white sheet of paper in his hand, reading. 'Thank you for your application and portfolio but we regret to inform you ... ' And then he just keeps reading that part over and over again, *we regret to inform you, we regret to inform you*, saying it as he crumples the paper up in a ball and drops it down into the creek, regret, regret, regret.

'Francie. I'll still drive you down, okay? I'll come back here and work, just for a bit and then I'll come down. Then we'll do everything, go to that Mexican place, whatever.'

But all she can hear is *regret, regret, regret*. 'Liar.'

'A few months tops, I promise.'

'Liar.'

Because it's easier. And he might be right next to her, but he's still all grey and she's over here in a galaxy of blue. Right next to each other but so far away.

Then Heck's between them, his shirt off, big hairy belly flopping around and he's still sweating. 'Okay, I'm ready, Slim.'

'For what?'

'C'mon, man, don't fuck around. You gotta show us.'

Francie remembers something about this, a million years back at the diner. 'Show us what?'

'Regret, regret, regret.' Slim's singing it, wandering back to the car, Heck and Francie trailing him, following the music of regret, Slim prancing ahead doing his Jethro Tull impersonation with an imaginary flute, the pied piper of regret.

He leads them around the back of the Dart, and there the three of them stand, staring down at the trunk. The look on Slim like some bad magician about to do his big trick. It was like that TV show she watched with her mom where they were opening a sealed tomb for the first time – all the excitement of what was inside, and then bullshit.

Slim puts the key in the trunk, a twist, and the whole thing comes open. All the grey of the world coming out. Francie watches it pour out of the trunk, onto the ground, staining all the blue back to grey.

Heck pukes immediately, like his stomach was on standby. At first Francie can only think it's a joke, like this pale naked man is going to jump out of the trunk yelling *surprise*. But she takes one look at Slim, one look at his forehead, smooth and dead, to know that everything is fucked. Nobody talks for a while, only Heck gagging.

'Who is it?'

'I dunno.'

'What happened to him?'

'I dunno.'

Older than them, but maybe not too much, brownish hair, not too tall. Lips drawn back, almost like a smile, and something dark around the throat, like another smile. This is the first dead thing Francie has ever seen in all her days on this planet, and it's not even really that bad. With the big poplars swinging back and forth above them, the water in the creek going by, it's almost peaceful. Almost like the four of them are just hanging out here together.

'I was just drivin around, comin back from the pawn shop, and there was the van pullin into the station, lights goin, and so I drive up, see what's happening. Pull up right alongside the thing, nobody inside, nobody around. So I get out, go around to the back and the doors are open and there it is.'

'And so you took it?'

'No, I swear to fuck, Francie, I was there lookin at it and then I was pullin into your driveway.'

'So what – it just appeared in your trunk?'

'I don't fuckin know. I mean I guess I put it there, but it's like I blacked out. I got that letter yesterday and it's like my brain just shut off. I mean who the fuck am I? I was up all night, got in this fight, sold the cameras and there it was – this fuckin dead guy, right in front of me. And I thought fuck it. I'll stay here, I'll go back to sellin weed or popcorn like fuckin Normando or whatever, it doesn't fuckin matter, because I'm not gonna do covers for *National Geographic* or art shows. I'll never get outta here. I'm just gonna end up in the back of a fuckin van. No name. Nothing.'

Slim sits on the ground next to Heck, who is holding his head between his legs. 'Aw, jinkies.' Heck spits. 'I thought it'd be cool. This isn't cool. He's dead, man. He's really dead.'

Francie stares right into the dead man's eyes. Just one of those faces, like they say about serial killers – could be anybody. Might've passed him in the mall, or sat next to him on the bus. Now none of that's there, nothing in the eyes. Like when she'd wake Slim up in his cabin, that brief moment when he hadn't returned from sleep. His brain would be reeling his soul in and for a second he'd be no one.

She says, 'So is this Milly's brother?'

'What?'

'At Top Hat, Dunc said – is this Lemmy?'

Slim groans and turns his head to look in the trunk. 'Maybe.'

'You never met him?'

'Milly had him out at that old farmhouse. Oh fuck.' He hugs himself, shivering in his T-shirt. 'What do we do with it?'

'The fuck should I know?'

'Please, Francie.' Hands knit together like he's begging or praying. 'Just tell me what to do.'

She sits down on the dirt, all three of them lined up against the fender. 'You give him back to the cops.'

'Fuck that – you crazy?'

'Give him to Milly then.'

'You are crazy. Jyrki fuckin Myllarinen – you know what he … his own fuckin parents – you have any idea what he'd do to me?'

'It's his brother.'

'We don't know that. Anyway, thanks to this asshole,' he slaps Heck, 'he's gonna think I *stole* the fuckin body. I'm fucked. And if I show up with some dead guy that isn't his brother, I'm fucked anyway.'

'So what then?'

'We'll split.'

'What?'

'The car's already packed. We'll head for Toronto.'

'I'm not going to Toronto with a dead body in the fuckin trunk, Slim!'

'Fuck!' He jumps to his feet and kicks the fender. Then kicks it again. And again. Then he kicks Heck, who rolls away. Slim moves away, kicking trees, kicking rocks, kicking anything in his way.

Francie stands and walks down the slope to the creek. Slim let the grey out of that trunk and it was grey again, grey everywhere, only worse this time because it had sunk its teeth in and wouldn't let go now. But looking down, her hands are still blue, and closing her eyes she can feel a shard in her heart pumping blue through her veins.

This is the picture she'd like of herself – blue Francie. Not like her magazines. Pictures and pictures and pictures of beautiful people in beautiful clothes in beautiful places. That's why a lot of people do it, she guesses – to live in that state of beauty. But everything is ugly. It's just about being seen. More than Dad peering over his paper to say *Good morning*, or Mom pretending to care when she says *How was your day, honey*, or your friends looking straight through you to see only what you can give them. It would just be nice to be seen, all of her, like Slim used to see her through his camera. But that dead look on that dead body is the dead look you get everywhere. The dead look even on Slim's face these days. It's only a matter of time before someone else drags you down. Blue Francie slowly becoming grey Francie.

Splash! A body hits the water and Francie looks up to the bridge to see Slim at the railing. Looking back to the water to see the body pop to the surface.

'What the fuck're you doing?'

'Getting rid of it!' Slim looking all pleased, like he's solved a problem, not ruined everything.

It's floating away, and she's following along the bank, pushing through the bushes, branches clawing at her face and hair, trying to keep it in sight. Slim yelling something stupid and pointless behind her. The body just going all peaceful, carried along by the creek. The path curves away and the brush is getting so thick she's going to lose it, so she steps into the water. She expects it to be needle cold, but she can't feel anything. She wades out into the middle of the creek, waist deep, so close she could touch it.

But then it's by and she's missed her chance. On it goes heading for the culvert where the creek runs under the road. The black mouth opening to swallow the body. Francie's voice shouting blue words, 'I can see you! I can see you!'

Slim's arms around her, pulling her back, Francie still fighting, trying to keep seeing. Both of them finally falling back on the shore. Slim crying. Francie just lying there, feeling the weight of each snowflake. Flake by flake covering them up, maybe even burying them.

She stands, brushes the snow off. Slim reaches for her. 'I'm ready. We can go. Let's go now.'

'No.' Because you can't pin your dreams on other people, like some kind of game of pin-the-tail-on-whatever. 'No.' Because she was that close, like the body floating by, close enough to touch, to see, and Slim and her, they both missed their chance. 'No.' Because way off over the trees, it almost looks like there's a little crack in the sky, a bit of blue starting to show.

And as she walks away, she looks for her smokes and finds the photo strip in her pocket. The four little squares of her still white, still waiting to be found.

4

Normando sits in one of those damned little gowns on the edge of the gurney, bare-ass except for his black socks. Bart sitting over there rubbing his chin and flipping through the charts. Normando staring out the window at the snow falling, first of the year. People clucking around out there – digging the winter clothes out, buying shovels, stringing up the tinsel, tossing salt all over the damned place – like they forget the first snow always melts. Same damned thing every year.

Bart finally lowers the paperwork and looks him in the eyes.

'It's spreading.'

Normando nods, already knowing this, feeling it inside these past few weeks, slow like peanut butter on bread.

'We said that was probably going to be the case, but now that we know.' He raises his eyebrows, letting that hang. 'Have you told Pat yet?'

'No.'

'She should know.'

He goes to a drawer and opens it, shuffling through more papers, coming back and shoving something at him. 'Take a look at these, then we'll have you back in for a chat. All right?'

'Right, Doc.'

The door half cocked, Bart turns back. 'You still running that cart around downtown?'

'Every damned day.'

'Well, good. Good to get some fresh air.' Bart waves his folder as he leaves, giving him one of those encouraging grins you save for the walking dead. 'Lots of options, Norm.'

The door closing and him left with a handful of pamphlets. A pamphlet for every day of the damned year left.

5

Milly's on the shitter when he hears the old man shrieking for Lemmy up on the porch. The noise goes on and on, so shrill it forces his asshole to pucker like a pair of old lips, trapping all that mess up inside him. He pulls his jeans up with one hand and kicks open the door to the outhouse.

The grass is crunchy with overnight frost and there's the skinny geezer out there in his socks and nothing else. His shrivelled cock slapping around as he yells his head off. Milly climbs the porch and throws his jacket around the old man's shoulders, only the grey bulb of his head popping out of all that flannel. Milly speaks softly into his ear, 'C'mon, Ukki, let's go inside.'

'*Ei, ei, et sinä.*' The old man shakes him off, going to the porch railing. The fields roll out before them, brown and tired and full of nothing again this year. 'Lemminki!' the old man yells, like he might come waddling out of the trees any minute with that stupid grin of his. Walk past the rusted tools, the barn falling into the ground, the purple tractor. The sun not even up yet and already Milly's too weary for this world.

'Väinö!' the old man tries, his voice cracking. 'Louhi!'

'Ukki.' Milly takes the old man's arm, thin like a wishbone in his hand, and gently pulls him away. But the old man latches onto the railing, throwing himself forward like the captain of a sinking ship.

'Väinö! Louhi! Lemminki!'

'They're gone, Ukki.' He scoops the old man up in his arms and carries him toward the house. 'It's just me.'

The old man looks at him, all hopeful with his big wet eyes. 'Lemminki?'

'No, it's me. Jyrki.'

'*Ei, ei.*' Giving him a look like this is all his fault. These dead fields. The rotting shingles. The paint peeling in strips. The old man's mind. Their family. The wind taking it all away. '*Ei, ei, et sinä,' not you, Jyrki Myllarinen, anybody but you.*

By the time Milly gets the old man all tucked under his electric blanket, he's already drifted off to some kind of sleep. He kisses him on the forehead, a faint taste of onion, and then shuts him away with a soft click.

He puts the kettle on and throws back the kitchen rug, the chain looped through the fat brass ring and a padlock holding the whole thing down. He uses the key around his neck, the chain purring out of the ring, then grabs a hold and pulls the trap door open. Seven-oh-one says the clock on the stove. Two minutes to daylight.

He goes one foot, feet together, one foot, inching down the steep set of stairs a lesson he learned after smacking his head one too many times. At the bottom he reaches out and feels for the steel door, running his hand down to find the lock. In goes another key, the door coming open with a whine. One minute left.

The heat hits him first and then that sickly sweet smell. He takes a step forward into that wet dark, the noise of the fans like some sleeping giant down here. He feels for the switch, counting down from ten, nine, eight, seven years since his parents died, six, five Lemmy's favourite number – high fives for getting yourself dressed in the morning, high fives for wiping your own ass – four, three days since he went off into the woods, three days waiting, two of them left, just him and the old man, one and almost there, teetering on the edge, counting down to zero, to Milly, to nothing. He flicks the switch. Sunrise.

The fluorescents *ting ting ting* on. The walls, ceiling, floor – everything splashed with white paint to reflect the light. Four rows of green. Greener than any crop he's tried to plant out in the fields the past few years. Plants taller than him – like him and Lemmy, children outgrowing their parents. He snaps on a pair of latex gloves, grabs a sack and walks the rows.

The buds are just forming, most of them reaching out with strands of white lace, but he finds a few males in the crop. He uproots these, gently so as not to disturb the little bell-like clusters, and shoves them away in the sack.

He checks the temp, the humidity, the water flow, the soil, he checks the fluorescent tubes, he checks and double-checks everything like he does every morning. It's going to be a good one, maybe the best yet – Väinö would never have believed it. Everything Milly touched turned to shit out in the field, he said. Little Ilmarinen, his father called him, with the golden touch. He'd grab Milly's hands and twist his palms up. *Look at these*, he'd say. *Soft hands, baby's hands like your mother.*

The kettle's going off upstairs. He grabs a jug of ethanol from the chemical cupboard. He leaves the lights on, locks the door, up the stairs, locks the trapdoor, rearranges the rug in the kitchen – makes sure everything is in order. Not for the cops, but so Lemmy doesn't get into it.

He pours a mug of mint tea, dipping the bag in and out because he hates waiting. Puts on his rubber boots and pulls on his itchy red flannel and heads back out into the cold, dropping the sack of uprooted plants on the porch as he goes.

The sun can't find a way through and the morning is coming up like a grey hangover on the hills. Milly walks the furrows. Here where Väinö ran spuds, here beans, here turnips – the best in Canada, he said. The seeds from the family farm in Espoo, smuggled over in the lining of Ukki's jacket when he came in on the boat from Finland. He'd help load up the truck in the middle of the night and tuck in between his parents on the dark road into the city, Lemmy on his lap. They'd set up their stall at the Borgia market, and Dad would give him a few nickels and tell him to take Lemmy for a walk. *Nobody wants to look at that when they're thinking about food*, he'd say.

Now the furrows are choked with weeds and maple saplings. He tried at first, but it didn't matter what he did, or how hard he worked at it. These last years he'd begun to find a strange happiness in watching things stunt, dry up, die. All the decades of work erased. Even the best turnips in Canada. Especially the turnips.

Lemmy loves the empty field. *It's like the ocean*, Milly said. *Why don't you sail on it?*

We're not asposed to, Yershey. Dad says.

Dad's not here, Lemmy. And he'd get him running over the furrows, a boat over the waves. Lemmy making motorboat sounds with his fat tongue hanging out, spitting all over the place. Both of them kicking dirt, running over the field like they were never allowed to, trampling it into a playground.

Milly follows the fence down to the end of the lot, finding a few holes that need patching, that needed patching last year. The land had been cleared by Ukki and Väinö years ago, and each spring Dad had been militant about hacking down or pulling up any vegetation that was creeping too close to his fence. Without him, the trees have slowly crowded in, reaching down to touch the posts, vines wrapping around from below, so close now the forest might climb right over and take it all back.

He stopped speaking Finn to Lemmy. Even castrated the two annoying dots off their last name. Of course, he keeps it from Ukki, he never wants to hurt the old man. Or Lemmy. Himself and the rest of the world, sure. If only he could dig up Väinö and show him how dead his dreams have become.

Something itches at the base of his neck and he's hit by the old crawling feeling of being watched. 'Lemmy?' he tries. There's a shape moving off in the deep woods. 'Lemmy!' and he's over the fence into the trees.

He's running, branches clawing at him, trying to slow him. He ducks under a low sweeping oak and pushes through a screen of tamarack, so close, right there, and then he trips on a log, rolling forward onto his back. The air knocked out of him. He chokes, coughing out white vapour.

Above him, the canopy of trees knits together and it's dark here, so dark. He props himself up on his elbows and sees it four, maybe five, feet away.

A fox.

Stopping to look at him, head cocked to the side, tongue poking out between teeth, almost the way Lemmy would. But it's not. He's been up and down every trail, driven every back road and patrolled the highway these past three days. Lemmy's gone.

The fox leaps over him and the trees swallow it up again.

Back over the fence, he picks up his mug where he left it and starts back for the house, then makes a detour to the tractor instead. Sitting in the middle of the field, rusting out. They painted it a few summers ago when Lemmy said his favourite colour was 'peeple.'

He swings himself up onto the seat, tucks the mug between his legs and gets both hands on the wheel. Lemmy liked to pretend it was the Batmobile and he was Batman. Milly was always Robin. The engine had long since been stripped for parts, but Lemmy would drive them all over the place from that one spot, clear across the country. Milly would pretend to fall off the tractor when they got to the Rockies, and this would always make his brother laugh. They'd finally get to the ocean and Lemmy would say, *Let's go swimming, Yershey.*

Can't, Lemmy.

Why not go swimming, Yershey?

Cause I forgot your water wings.

Yershey.

We'll have to go back for them. And Lemmy'd chase him into the house.

The machine smells like gasoline, even now. As if they could just drive off like Lemmy always wanted.

The tires at the back have started to sink into the dirt, like even the tractor is giving up. Väinö loved talking about the time Milly drove it into a ditch. *Well,* he said smoking a cigarette and looking down at it in the muck, *you'll never be a farmer, that's for sure.* He'd tell the story whenever Milly's friends were around. He'd say, *And you think the other one's a retard.* Nobody ever laughed except him.

He sucks at the cold mint tea and looks at the squat log house, so small now but somehow they used to fit in there, all of them, with all their yelling and all their silence.

Back up on the porch, he brings the clothesline in and takes down the plants he hung up to dry last week. He replaces these with the fresh plants from the sack and heads inside.

He puts a pot on the stove and fills it partway with ethanol, flicking on the burner. Then he cracks the stalks of the dried plants and shoves everything into the food processor.

He's just transferring the pulp into the pot when the phone rings.

'Yeah?'

'Milly?'

'Yeah.'

'It's Dunc.'

'I know.'

'Yeah – yeah, cool. Um … any news?'

Milly waits.

'Nothing, hey? Listen, this could totally be bogus – I mean, the source is legit, but you never know, right? But you said if I heard anything, and I just thought, y'know – '

'What is it, Duncan?'

'Yeah, um, well, I heard a body got brought in today. Early. Picked up off 17, out your way.'

The ethanol is starting to bubble, the air going thick with the sharp and the sweet. 'Is it him?'

'It could be anybody, Milly, I wouldna called but you said – '

'Is it him?' The words hissing out, his insides boiling like the pot.

'I dunno, nobody's saying anything, but it was out on 17 so I thought – '

'Meet me in Memorial Park, the usual place, a couple hours.'

'But, Milly – '

He drops the phone back on the cradle. His head spinning. He grabs the pot, a bubbling golden mess, the fumes overpowering, and dumps the whole thing down the drain. Some of the ethanol splashes up, burning into him, his insides burning out, and he kicks open the front door, pulling his shirt off to get at the cold. He finds the railing and tries to shout, to stop him, to say, *Wait, wait, I'm sorry, I didn't mean it, we'll go, we'll go all the way to the ocean.*

Then the old man's at his side, pale and naked again. He takes Milly's hand, curling arthritic fingers around his. He turns toward the forest and yells, 'Lemminki!'

And they shout together, over and over, until there are no words left for what they've lost.

He feeds the old man buttered porridge and then gets him back in bed. Milly kisses him on the forehead again, then once, light on the lips. The way Lemmy always does. As he gets up, those strong bony hands catch him again.

'What is it, Ukki?'

From under the covers, the old man brings a headless doll. Lemmy's favourite toy, Moomin. The day Lemmy brought it to him with the head snapped off, crying, *I killed it, Yershey.*

It's a just a toy, Lemmy.

I killed Moomin, Yershey.

Toys can't die, Lemmy, only people die.

Why does it got to get killed, Yershey? Big tears coming down his face. And Milly knew he wasn't just talking about the toy anymore.

'Jyrki.' The old man pushing the doll into his chest. As Milly closes the door, the last thing he sees are his eyes. So wide and young you'd never know the mind behind them was gone.

They used to share Lemmy's bedroom, but now Milly sleeps in their parents' old room. The bunk beds are still there, though, with the seahorse comforter and the little happy-faced moon nightlight and if you didn't know it you'd think some kid lived in here, not a grown man.

Milly stands in the doorway, about to toss the doll on the bed, but is stopped by one of his old posters on the wall. A picture of dozens of sailboats on the water, snow-capped mountains behind them – *Come to Vancouver.*

Vancoomer, Lemmy would say, *the oh shine, Yershey.*

Ocean, it's one word, Lemmy.

And there was a picture pinned to the cork bulletin board, done in pencil crayon. Two round dots in a half moon, purple squiggles behind them. Jyrki and Lemmy in the ocean.

On his way out, he stops in his bedroom, goes into the closet and reaches high up to pull the Pystykorva off its hook. He bends down on one knee, pops the magazine, blows into it, replaces it and pulls the bolt back. The way Ukki showed him, out in the fields. Only taking him this far, never pulling the trigger. He makes sure the safety's on and slings it over his shoulder.

He makes his way out to the two tarp-covered mounds sitting in the driveway. He yanks the sheet off the first one. The Barracuda. Coal black and polished like a razor. He slides into the driver's seat and gets the key turned. Nothing. Turns again. More nothing. He took it out just last week and she was purring then.

When he slides back out he sees it. Gas cap off and a hose dangling. It clicks. The smell of gasoline at the tractor. Lemmy'd tried to drive off like Batman and probably spilled gas all over the place doing it.

Not going to waste time trying to siphon it back. Tarp's off the second mound. The Beetle. Yellow paint and rust. Dragged by a crane out of the bottom of a ravine. They wanted to take it to the junkyard, but he said no. Washed out the stains, put in a new windshield, hammered the hood back into shape. Never could bring himself to repaint it. Yellow her favourite colour.

He tosses the Pystykorva and the doll on the passenger seat. It hasn't been driven since, only started up once a year. But even with stale gas, the engine comes to life on the first try. Figures.

He drives the curving dirt road and rolls up to the edge of the highway. The asphalt stretching out in either direction. Right and he's going into the city – going after Lemmy, going back to the farm, back to the plants, back to Ukki, back to his parents' grave, back to tending and caring and bathing and feeding, back to going along the long flat line of life.

Then there's left. On to the Soo, on to Thunder Bay, on to the badlands and on up the mountains and on and on to the coast. To the ocean. The farm behind him. Ukki, Lemmy, the sad dead city – everything far behind. Tomorrow and all the days on and on – his. Just like all the pictures he'd scissored out of magazines and stuck on the walls of his bedroom, like the ocean behind his eyelids. Finally his.

A snowflake. Just one, falling so slow. First of the year. He follows it down to the hood of the car where it melts. And then another. Second of the year and another, the third, and another, and more, losing count. Here comes another hard winter.

Or he could stay here. The car'll be buried under snow and he can hibernate until spring.

The Pystykorva on the seat next to him. Running his hand down the oiled barrel, the wood stock, catching at the slash cut into the butt of the rifle. Ukki had carved one notch there, carved it so deep you could see daylight on the other side. He was no expert sniper. Not like Simo Häyhä, Ukki said, no *valkoinen kuolema.* No White Death – *ei, ei, et sinä*, not him. Carved this one notch down in some ditch over the ocean and then never moved on. Bringing that one notch with him over the ocean, into the house he built, and passing it on to his son, his grandsons, putting it into the fields around them. Milly stuck with this inheritance of the dead and dying.

He puts the car into gear and turns right. Going on, because sometimes that's enough to get you through the day. Going gone.

The highway is a long black tongue all the way from Spanish, leading Milly down into the belly of the city.

He drives in a trance. The windshield wipers keeping the snow off, each slow pass pulling back another curtain in his brain. Lemmy hit by a transport out on the road. Lemmy freezing out in the forest. Lemmy attacked by wild animals. Lemmy slipping, hitting his head on a rock. Lemmy falling in the river. The many ends of Lemmy.

He's just on the other side of McKerrow when he spots the ravine. Deep and wet like a mouth on his left side. He doesn't know the exact spot. By the time Ukki took them there, the road crews had cleaned everything up, replaced the guardrails. He always figures he'll feel something different on this patch of road.

He had packed a bag before he went to sleep that night. The decision finally made. He only told Lemmy, before he climbed into his bunk, *I'll come back for you.*

He'd been lying in bed waiting, not knowing what for, when the phone rang. It rang and rang so much he was afraid Lemmy would wake up, but he slept through anything and Ukki's hearing was already gone and mind going at that point. He let it ring until the sun came through the trees and then he walked out to the kitchen and picked it up and said hello like you would with any phone call and somebody told him how sorry she is to tell him.

When Mom came into their rooms earlier that night she kissed Lemmy first, and then she climbed up to his bunk and leaned in. Väinö yelling from the kitchen, 'Let's go!' Her breath coming out sour with alcohol. This is what they would say later, that she was drunk, but he knew that wasn't it. That's not what sends a car through a guardrail at the speed of light. *Take care of your brother* was the last thing she said to him. It was the only powerful thing he'd ever known her to do.

He tries to imagine them in that moment, that split second of flight. If they felt free. If there had been room for a sliver of warmth. A look to say, *So this is all we've been.* Or if there was still only room for one final gush of violence. *Take care of your brother,* like he hadn't been doing that since the day he was born. But he took it on like everything else. *A pack mule*, Dad used to say, *Not good for anything else but carrying paska.* Shit. He left his bag packed, just in case.

To him it just looks like another ravine and he never slows down, not even with the snow trying to claw him back.

Duncan's waiting for him on the steps of the cenotaph in the park. His hood's up, but a bit of green mohawk pokes out at the front like a horn. He's watching the traffic and twitching all over the place.

'You look like a junkie, Duncan.'

'It's fuckin cold, man.'

'Let's take a walk.'

They follow the path, through the trees, Duncan kicking at rocks with his combat boots. 'So, um, how's things out in Spanish?'

Milly looks at Duncan, giving him time to stop asking stupid questions. He steps over the legs of some drunk passed out under a bush.

They get to the playground and Milly drops himself into a swing. Duncan stands around, playing with the chain on his belt, looking one way, the other, anywhere except into Milly's eyes. Like some kid dressed up for Halloween, too small for his costume.

'Fuckin snow, eh?' He tries a laugh that turns into a cough and then spits, getting some on the sleeve of his leather jacket. Wiping it on his pants. 'So my guy was in this morning, busted for carrying – Josh, you know Josh, right?' Duncan's eyes flick up, trying to read him, but he still gives the kid nothing. 'Yeah, um, so Josh says these two cops come running in, saying they just found this body out on 17 and they got it in the back of their van.'

'I already heard this.'

'Yeah, I just thought you'd like the whole – '

'Is it him?'

'I dunno, Milly.'

Milly jumps out of the swing and starts to cut across the lawn. Duncan jogs to catch up, trailing after.

'Where're you goin?'

'To the station.'

'What? What for?'

'To get him.'

'But – you can't.'

'Why?'

'That's what I'm tryin to tell you, Milly – fuck. He's gone.'

Milly stops and looks at Duncan, shoulders hunched up, the kid's nose dripping snot. For a second, he's about to reach out and crush his throat. He sees the bulge of Duncan's larynx crawl as he swallows and his fingers imagine the shape, squeezing, squeezing, and the rattle that follows.

Instead he pulls a handkerchief out of his back pocket and tosses it. 'Wipe your nose.'

Duncan dabs at his dripping nose, looking all apologetic. 'Josh said that when they went out to the van to get him, he'd disappeared – somebody took him.'

'Who?'

'I'm not sure.'

'Duncan.' He says it quiet, but he feels the edge come into his voice, the words walking a razor.

'Uh, I heard this guy at the arcade – his friend – blabbing about this body in the trunk and – '

'Duncan.' So quiet the kid's eyes bulge, looking at Milly the way a lot of people look at him. Fear. The way they all used to look at Väinö. Because you never knew if he was going to cut you or kiss you. Or which one was worse.

'Slim Slider. You know Slim – he worked for you a while back, right?'

'Where?'

'What're you gonna do?'

He knows the stories they tell and he's not sure if people are afraid of him because of what he's done or what he's capable of doing. 'I'm going to talk to him.'

'I dunno where he is – he was at the arcade and then – '

'When?'

'Bout an hour ago.'

'Where did he go?'

'I dunno, man. He could be anywhere. He drives a red Dart – I know that.'

He nods. It's a start. He walks over to the chain-link fence closing off the pool. The pit all dried up, filled with leaves. The seal sculpture at the far end. In the summer, water spouts from the seal's mouth.

'Uh, Milly?' Duncan at his shoulder again. 'I gotta get back.'

'Yeah.'

But he doesn't go anywhere and Milly can feel him twitching away beside him. 'Just wondering if … ' He trails off, wipes at his nose. 'You bring, uh, anything with you?'

He turns his head, just enough for the kid to know that this is not the thing to ask. Disgusting to even think about business here. Now.

'Yeah, cool. Be seeing you.'

He turns back to the pool and doesn't even notice Duncan leave. Mom used to bring them here when they were kids. He grew out of it pretty quick, but even now he'd drive Lemmy in every weekend until the pool closed in September. If they got here when the right lifeguard was on, she wouldn't say anything about Lemmy being too old or too big. He'd spend hours in the water, until his lips were blue, and even then he'd refuse to come out.

But in the water he was sleek and graceful. He shivered like an otter. All the awkwardness of his low, squat body released. He'd pop out spitting water. *The oh shine, Yershey.* In the water he was free.

He leaves the park and cuts across the street. Walking slow and letting the cars stop for him.

He pulls open the door to the Nickel Bin and ducks inside. He lets his eyes adjust – like a cave in here, wet and dark, and it's only when the thick wall of day-old cigarette smoke hits him that he remembers where he is.

The bartender, Foisey, is leaning with his back against the bar, watching the television above him. Milly scans the rest of the place – pudgy guy with a moustache dressed in black setting up equipment on the small stage, off in the corner some other guy he maybe recognizes from the old days sleeping on a table. Nothing else but shadows. He walks up and takes a stool at the bar.

'Tea. Please.'

Foisey gives him a glance and then comes back hard. He closes his mouth pretty quickly and tries to play it off with a nod. He goes to plug the kettle in. Milly pretends he can't feel the stare reflected in the mirror behind the bar.

'You know a kid named Slim?'

Foisey keeps his back to him. 'Slim? Nope, sorry.' But a twitch of his neck gives him away.

'You see all that snow out there?' It's the guy with the moustache, sitting down next to him with a coffee. Milly gives him a quick nod, keeping his eyes on Foisey's back. 'The same every year – first snow and everybody forgets how to drive.' He takes off his hat and rubs the sweat off his bald head, snapping the hat back down quick like something might escape. 'Jyrki Myllarinen, right?'

Milly shifts his eyes, taking this guy in. Grey in his moustache, older than he looks. 'Yeah.'

'I used to teach your brother piano.'

Milly's memory stirs – this guy, Bedard, one of Mom's efforts, have Lemmy play piano because that's what normal kids do. 'Oh yeah.' Palms and fingers fumbling together over some kind of handshake.

'How's he doin?'

'Fine, fine.'

'Good kid.'

'Yeah, Lemmy's great.' Lemmy banging away on their piano. *Practising,* Mom called it. Always happy making a racket and he suddenly feels he owes this sad-eyed man something.

'So, what're you doing these days?'

'Well, still playing. Playing here tonight. Big reunion concert.'

'That right?'

'Yep. Have to see who turns up. Big deal, I guess.'

'Yeah.' Trying to remember what band, what kind of music. 'You guys were … something.'

'Yeah, well … thanks, lad. We had our time, I guess. Toured Europe – parts of it anyway. Even played with Downchild at the El Mo once. Almost got that record contract. Almost.' He takes a slurp of his coffee, holding it in his mouth all thoughtful, like it was the best kind of Scotch. 'Guess there's some dreams that never die, eh? Or you die with em.'

'Yeah, guess so.'

Foisey puts a steaming cup of tea in front of him. He sips at it, the guy next to him sipping too – one of them dipping down while the other pulls back.

Milly thinks about that night, him in bed listening to his parents scream again, dropping down out of his bunk to pack his suitcase. Then the guardrails and the car flying. After that the bag stayed packed for seven years and all those dreams of the coast packed away with it and Lemmy saying, *Tell me bout the oh shine, Yershey.* Parcelling out those dreams, stretching them like taffy over seven years for them to live off the fumes. Seven years of bringing his coast, Milly's coast, back to life over and over again. Passing on his dream like a disease to Lemmy until even that isn't his anymore and then three days ago Lemmy says, *Tell me bout the oh shine, Yershey* and he says, *What, Lemmy, what, what in the hell do you want to know?*

Where's the oh shine, Yershey?

Out west. In Vancouver.

Can we go to Vancoomer, Yershey?

No.

Why not?

Because.

Why not go?

Because we can't.

Why not go? Why not?

We can't, Lemmy.

Why not?

Because it's gone.

No, Yershey.

And out comes the suitcase and he's opening it and throwing clothes around and screaming at Lemmy the way his parents screamed at each other, the way he promised himself he'd never scream at anyone. *It's gone, you stupid retard. All dried up – the whole ocean – all of it. Gone, all gone. Like Mom and Dad and Ukki and me and everything*. Gone.

And when he wakes, Lemmy and the suitcase are gone too.

'Well, I gotta get back. Young minds to ruin.' The stool shrieking as the guy pushes back, zipping up his leather jacket. He sticks out his hand for another awkward shake. 'You should come by tonight – it's gonna be just like old times.'

'Maybe. I've got someone to take care of first.' And when Bedard gives him a weird look, he forces his lips into a little smile and finishes, 'My brother.'

Milly turns back to the bar, done talking. Behind him, he feels the guy take the hint and leave. Now just him and Foisey. Milly pictures his brother all laid out, his eyes closed, stuffed in the trunk of some car. Somebody driving who doesn't give two shits about Lemmy. About where he belongs.

Foisey has his back turned again, polishing beer glasses like the world depends on it. Milly clears his throat. 'Where can I find him?'

'Who?'

'Where,' taking a sip, slowing this down to make sure he's heard, 'can I find him?'

'Listen, man, I don't know the kid.'

Milly watches Foisey in the mirror as he dips his teabag in and out of the mug, letting the silence sit, smelling the stink of the other man's nerves.

'Where can I find him?'

'What the fuck d'you want with him anyway?'

Milly feels the words come up from his gut, flopping heavy onto the bar for Foisey to see. 'Where can I find him?'

The glass Foisey is polishing breaks and he breathes in sharply, grabbing at his hand. 'Look – I know his mother. She works over at that cop diner on Larch.' He wraps the towel around his hand.

Milly takes one final sip and puts a dollar bill on the counter. 'Thanks for the tea.'

As Milly pushes through the door he bumps into someone coming in. A big fella, half a foot taller than him. Head like a brick. Familiar. Wiping blood off his face with a sleeve. Just a bump, an inch of skin, and normally he'd give this guy a look to fuck off, but that inch gives him a chill like his grave's been trampled all over. Or maybe it's just this day he's stepping out into. This day that started three days ago with Lemmy walking off.

He stands on the steps outside the Nickel Bin. The snow is laid out so white and pure you almost forget the city underneath it. Almost forget that by tomorrow everything will be grey sludge kicked up by cars.

A squeaking and here comes some cart rolling down the street. Normando pushing his popcorn cart. He hasn't been down here for he doesn't know how long and it's all the same. That scrawny crow as ancient now as he was years ago. When Mom used to make them cross the street when they saw Normando coming. Nothing ever changes. Same potholes, same burnt-out street lights, same graffitied brick, same sad-faced businessmen, same whores on Elgin, same Normando pushing that same cart same time every morning heading for the same corner. Nothing changes. He's only been in the city for an hour and already he feels it leaning in on him from all corners like it always did, and he just wants to be free of it. The city, yeah, but all the rest too.

The clouds are moving above him. Layers and layers of grey crawling over one another. Grey for days on end. But for a moment, a hole opens, clouds shifting to allow a single patch of blue. Vibrant. And he thinks about lying in the top bunk and Lemmy saying, *Tell me bout the oh shine, Yershey.* And he wouldn't yell, he'd tell him about water and whales and sailboats and submarines and starfish and coral reefs and mountains and the people you'll meet, good people and the space, oh god, so much space. Above them a galaxy of glow-in-the-dark stickers across the ceiling.

Can we go Yershey?

Yes.

Today Yershey?

Yes, today, Lemmy.

And they'd be free. Free in the ocean. Free from their awkward bodies and histories. From this hard unforgiving sidewalk slab. Free. His feet are coming off the ground and he's falling slowly up toward that blue, Lemmy beside him smiling. Looking back to see the city fading out. Floating up so high he's leaving behind the dead farm in Spanish, Ukki waving from the porch, the wreck of their parents' car. High over everything, finally splashing into all that blue. Like Lemmy in the water. Free. Released.

Then crashing back to that patch of miserable concrete outside the bar and he looks up to see Lemmy going up and up. Leaving him like everyone leaves him, to deal with the mess. Leaving him behind. Going on. Going gone.

6

Normando pushes the damned cart, *squeaksqueak, squeaksqueak*, down Durham to the corner of Larch. Sets up right underneath the yellow canopy of the news shop. People walk by. Businessmen going to work, hookers going to bed. It's a morning routine. The way a downtown shakes off sleep like some old dog.

Light the propane, wipe the kettle and in with the wad of lard like a baby into a cradle. One, two, three. Hands into the sack. *Quatre, cinq, six*. Coming out with gold. Seven, eight, nine. He opens the mouth of the kettle and, *dix*, the kernels rattle in like broken teeth. He pours salt over it all.

There's the sizzle. This crowded moment in the morning, just before the sun clears the smudgy brick buildings, just before the first bargain hunters tramp down the cracked pavement to Woolworth's or the bins at Liberty, before the men slouch around the barbershops. This instant before the damned day cracks wide open.

Here it comes. *Pop*. The smell of summer. Even as the first snow falls around him. Carnivals. *Pop*. Midways. *Pop*. Baseball games in old weedy fields. *Pop pop*. Movie theatres with busted springs and sticky floors. *Pop pop pop*.

The day spilling out from all sides. No stopping it now. No way to hold it to that moment. To pin it down like a butterfly in some damned display case, as close to perfect as a dead thing can get.

He's got his regulars, but he never sells that much. Just enough to get by on. It started as a weekend thing, while he was paying off the mortgage. Then when the mine was done with him and his bad knees, he started coming down on those same bad knees every day. Gets him away from the house and that gaggle of women Pat has in and out all damned day. Chattering about their damned kids. Chattering about the kids their damned kids've had. And on and on. The things people leave after them. Careless. Scattered like seed to be gobbled up.

Thirty years he's been popping now, he figures.

Still, he hears the whispers. He sees the men laugh to each other, pretending to gag. He sees the mothers pull their children close or cross the street. They don't like his smile. But he's part of the day. And they count on him being there. Like they used to count on the old clock tower in the post office. Before they swung a wrecking ball and brought it all low. Just another hole down here now. Like pulling out your own guts and trying to live empty. They still need something to orbit around. Some cities got statues the birds shit on, and he's the next best thing.

He pours in the last batch at four, stretches it like taffy through the hour. The last few bags he gives out to some hungry characters on their way to or from the Sally Ann.

He doesn't touch the stuff himself. The years have told him it don't fill you up, no matter how much you eat. So he lives off the smell. The ghost of something better.

Squeaksqueak, squeaksqueak. Back down the street, in time to catch the businessman heading home and the hookers coming out of the alleys. The damned deep voice of church bells up and down the streets.

The old dog settles down. Waits for his return. He brings the day with him when he goes.

7

It's the too-familiar smell of rotten eggs that brings her back to where she is and what she's doing. Here in the plastic bucket seat in Mario's. Her hair's all up in rods but in the mirror she can tell her face is falling down. Creases, wrinkles and lines, everything deeper today than yesterday than the day before. Forty-three next month and Martha Novak is looking at another hard winter.

'So who's the lucky guy this time?' Lucy back in the salon chair, Mario's hairy knuckles working out the dye job in the sink. Martha butts out her second-last cigarette, thinking, Least I don't have any grey yet.

'William something – no, Walter.'

'What's he do?'

'I dunno. Velma's brother knows him. Wife died.'

'A widower. I like sad men. They're quiet.'

Martha drops her magazine. She read it last time she was in and the time before that. 'I don't even know why I put myself through it.'

Mario stops washing Lucy's hair. He points his comb at Martha. 'You need to find the nice man.' Nice, like the word means something. Something other than Frank the insurance salesman who liked to go for steak dinners and always split the tab. Or Lorenzo the janitor who talked only about the woman who left him and never mentioned his daughter. Or old Tom Frost who was still married, still living with his wife, but soon, soon, someday. Or Felix, or Hank, or James, or the other men. Nice, what you reach at the end of words.

'You put yourself through it so you don't end up alone.'

'I'm not alone.'

'Don't talk to me about that boy of yours – him out all hours of the day and night. He was in at the restaurant this morning bragging about some stuff he pawned at Oz's.'

'What stuff?'

'For drugs probably. Or booze.'

'He doesn't touch that shit.'

'Oh, don't be an idiot. He'll move out someday – soon – and what'll you have? A big empty apartment.'

'I like being alone.'

'No you don't.' Lucy shakes water off like a drowning rat, while Mario attacks her with a towel. 'No one does. The worst thing in the world. Any one of em is better than that.'

Martha picks up another magazine she's already read and starts to re-reread an article about all the new things that give you cancer. Behind her, Mario hums opera as he washes out Lucy's hair, stopping to look at the television, stopping to chat, stopping to touch his moustache in the mirror, stopping to take the espresso pot off the hot plate, stopping so often that he might never finish washing Lucy's hair.

'Mario, can you get this out before my hair goes purple already?' Lucy thrashes around to see Mario peering out the window. 'Fuck's sake, Martha, it's snowing.'

Martha looks up from her magazine. Outside, snowflakes fat and slow are coming down, still space enough for people to dodge between. A couple walks by, the man's arm thrown across the woman's shoulders, pulling her close, her burrowing into his chest, getting ready for the winter.

Mario turns at the window, points his comb at Martha. 'A man say nice things but he not the nice man.'

Martha with her perm and Lucy with her black-almost-purple hair under the awning of Mario's shop, Martha smoking her second-last cigarette and watching the barber pole spin.

'Just like it to snow today.' Lucy looks at the sky, the universe against her. 'So where're you meeting this guy?'

'The Empress.'

'Ooh, cultured. When?'

'Bout a half-hour.'

'Perfect. Enough time to grab a beer.'

'It's not even noon.'

'C'mon, help you loosen up.' Lucy pulls Martha off down the street, both of them rushing with a hand up like some small shield to protect their new hair. Martha tries to picture what a Walter would look like and if it matters anyway. Long face, droopy eyes, bad sweater.

They pass Normando pushing his popcorn cart, Lucy giving him a dirty look and whispering to Martha, 'You know he picks his nose.' Martha tries to shush her but Lucy mimes jamming a finger up her nose, like Martha needs the image. One of the wheels going squeaky on him as Normando pushes that thing down the street to the corner. The same corner. And Martha almost turns and goes back to buy a bag of popcorn, nose picking or not, to thank him for being there year after year. For sticking around.

'Ain't that your boy over there?' Lucy pointing across the intersection and Martha sees Slim coming up Elm, the collar of his jacket flipped up against the weather.

'Slim honey!' He stops and looks around, spots her across the street and cringes. She shouldn't've said *honey* and she shouldn't wave but she does anyway. 'Honey, I work at four, but I'll leave some dinner on the stove.' But he's already moving, crossing on the red and away. Martha eventually brings her hand down.

'Where'd he get those fancy things?'

'What?'

'The boots. Putting them all over the furniture at the restaurant.'

Martha looks down at the water Slim's kicking up and sees the dark brown leather cowboy boots on his feet. She's never seen them before but they look familiar anyway.

'Thinks he's Randolph Scott or something,' Lucy snorts.

Martha flicks her cigarette, the white nub buoyed by the melting snow and then dragged down into the storm drain. 'Well, maybe I'll get him spurs for his birthday.'

'Why not a goddamn horse while you're at it. Be your regular knight in shining armour. Not like his deadbeat father.'

'Lucy.'

'I'm just saying – the apple don't fall far from the vine. What's this business with that boy changing his name anyway?'

'His name?'

'Yeah, he's going by Slim *Slider* now. Is that his ... his gang name?'

Martha looks back up the street toward the small figure of her son, just like a little boy at this distance. 'That's my maiden name.'

'Oh.' Lucy shifts her purse awkwardly. And then laughs – hard, fake, an of-course-I-knew-that laugh. 'Well, whatever name he's trying to hide behind, he's gonna turn out just like his father.'

'Van'll be back.'

'Fuck's sake, Martha.' And she heads down the sidewalk, yelling over her shoulder. 'Van Novak ran out on you just like that boy's gonna.'

'He'll be back.' But she says it just quiet enough while Lucy's walking ahead that no one can say any different.

Lucy's wheezing by the time they climb the stairs at the Empress and step onto the thick red carpet. Paper lanterns, the smell of oil and fish. Jean leads them to a booth in the back, one of the ones where you sit on a cushion on the floor. Lucy doesn't even bother with a menu. 'Take a Northern.'

Martha sits with a clear view to the stairs. 'I'll have a tea, Jean, thanks.'

'Fuck that, she'll have a Northern too.'

'No, really.'

'Yes, really.'

Jean disappears behind a curtain. Lucy crosses her legs and places her palms face up on her knees, starts humming.

'Lucy, stop it.'

'What? I'm doing some yogi.' She rolls her head from side to side, as always enjoying the performance, even more since she played the mayor's wife in that amateur production of *Bye Bye Birdie* last year. 'How're you gonna know it's him?'

'Who?'

'Willy.'

'Walter. I dunno, Velma didn't say.'

'Ugh, that's never a good sign.' Lucy brushes imaginary crumbs off the tablecloth. 'You should let me set you up again.'

'No.' A few dismal nights resurfacing. Men Lucy met working at Gloria's.

'What? Didn't you like that Indian dentist I found for you?'

'Prabir. He's a psychiatrist.'

'What was wrong with him?'

'Nothing.' Martha plays with the edge of her placemat, a cheap piece of paper with the Chinese zodiac printed on it. Year of the dragon, year of the rat, year of the monkey. That monkey looking all pleased with himself. That big goofy grin she's seen before.

'Bet he did yogi. They don't eat pork, right?'

'I dunno. He was a Catholic.'

'Don't know how you could live without pork chops. Pork chops and dill.'

The curtain shivers and Jean comes back through, putting two cold glasses of golden ale on the table. Lucy shakes some salt into her glass, watches the nest of bubbles rise to the surface.

'What about that hockey player I seen you talking to?'

And for a second it's like she's back there at centre ice in the Arena. Him skating down the wing, flashing her a mouthful of broken teeth. The whipcrack sound of one body hitting another and then the entire stadium gone silent.

'What'd they used to call him – Spider?'

'Python.'

'Why?'

'Cause he used to crush people.'

'Ooh, I like that. He looks kinda like Paul Newman.'

'Paul Newman if his face'd been run over by the zamboni. Anyway, we're friends.'

'Friends?' Lucy saying it like a dirty diaper. 'Now that's a man that can take care of you.'

'We grew up together.'

'Nice butt too.' Lucy takes a big gulp of beer and belches, waving her hand in front of her mouth like she's waving away the conversation. 'You hear bout the dead guy they brought in this morning?'

'What? Where?'

'At the station. Found him out off 17. Naked, can you believe that?' Lucy titters, The scandal, oh the scandal.

'Who is he?'

'Dunno. Nobody said yet. Gotta watch the obituaries.' Lucy looking up as she sips her beer, that quick glance because she knows Martha already checks every day.

A man in an overcoat reaches the top of the stairs. Tie, briefcase – government man. Smiling at someone at a far table. Not alone, not a Walter.

'So what's he do, this Walter?'

'Uh, can't remember, transport driver or something.'

'Huh. You shoulda stayed with that doctor.'

'I didn't want to.'

'Why? You said there's nothing wrong with him.'

'I know, it's just – '

As Jean's walking by with a tray full of food, Lucy pinches her sleeve and leans out in that not-to-be-a-bother way. 'Can you bring me an eggroll, please, thanks.' Then back to Martha. 'Trust me, Herman's a pain in the arse, but he'll keep me warm this winter and it's gonna be a cold one.'

'There's nobody interesting left in this town.'

'Don't be ridiculous.'

'It's just … ' Martha pulling out her pack with nervous fingers and lighting her second-last cigarette. 'It's Van.'

Lucy puts her glass down hard. 'Fuck's sake, Martha.' She puts one hand on the table and leans back to look at the ceiling.

'I know, I know.' Martha's puffing little gasps, hardly inhaling. 'But I just keep thinking he's gonna kick open that old screen door and come on in.'

Two more men come up the stairs, looking back and forth, unsure whether to sit or wait or maybe leave. Mid-thirties – too young. Not a Walter. Not a Van.

Lucy leans forward, here comes the crown attorney. 'It's been seven years.'

'I know.'

'Seven years!'

'I know, don't you think I know?'

'Those weren't the days of roses – you couldn't agree on nothin and you bitched at each other all the time, I mean what's to miss?'

'There was more to it than that.'

'Your memory's goin.' She puts her hand on top of Martha's. 'Look, I just want to see you happy.' But Martha's not sure if this is still part of the performance.

Jean drops off the eggroll as she passes. Lucy splits the wooden chopsticks and starts rubbing them together, looking the part. Martha checks her watch, already past the hour. 'He's not coming.'

'That's what I keep telling you.'

'No, this guy – Walter.'

'Give em a chance.' She drops the eggroll three times and then just uses her fingers instead.

'Who'd they find, Lucy?'

'What?'

'Who'd they find dead on the highway?'

'I told you – I dunno. All Louise told me is they brought him in this morning, no identification.'

'Who is it?'

'I know what you're thinking.' Bean sprouts hanging out of her mouth. 'But it's not him.'

'You don't know that.'

'You know what you are, Martha – *obsessed*.' Waving the dying inch of her eggroll like a sceptre. 'And if it is him – y'know what? I'd be glad. Because maybe then you could get some closure – closure on these last seven years, closure on the whole thing.' Closure like some sort of buzzword she heard on Donahue last week and been dying to use, closure like the screen door banging when Van walked out of it that day he got into his car and took off for the store, closure like the screen door banging when Slim walks out of it every morning, screen door banged so much the hinge's gone off and it doesn't close at all anymore, hangs open just that little bit, just enough to let the ants in, like the screen door on her insides hanging halfway between open and closed. That monkey smiling up at her from the placemat, wrinkling as she drops a couple of tears down onto its stupid face. Just a couple to let her know she's still got them.

'I want to go see him.'

Lucy spitting eggroll. 'What?'

'I need to see if it's him.'

'Fuck's sake, Martha, we are not going down to the police station so you can look at a dead person. That's sick, is what it is. Now sit down, wipe your face and get ready for a nice lunch with a nice man.'

'He's not coming.' The staircase is silent, the few lunchers starting to head back to work. 'Nobody's coming.'

'Could you just wait.'

'Sure.' Martha grabs her purse. 'It's all I do.' Leaves her there with the two pints and all that grease on her lips.

Out into the snow, down Elm and over Lisgar and on down Larch to the police station, up to the counter where Martha stands until the thick-necked officer gives her the now-what look and says, 'Yeah?'

'I'm here to see the body.'

'Who?'

'The body that came in this morning from 17.'

'Ma'am.' He takes off his glasses like this is causing him some extreme pain. 'I don't know where you heard that, but I can't discuss the details of a criminal investigation.'

'That's fine. I don't want to discuss it, I want to see it.'

'Ma'am, are you a reporter?'

'No, I'm … I'm the wife.'

'Ma'am.' That word having less and less kindness to it. 'You can wait to see if the detective'll talk to you, but it'll be a while.' He nods at the plastic chairs against the wall.

'I'm not waiting.' She fights to keep her voice steady. Breathe.

'Ma'am, I'm going to ask you to step away from the counter.'

'I'm not.' And she turns and walks back down the hallway, stopping halfway, next to the coffee maker, leaning against the wall thinking, I can't go back. I can't go on.

'Heard you talking to Officer Friendly back there.' A smile. A short man pouring coffee in a styrofoam cup, tossing whitener into it. Blue uniform pants, white undershirt. Salt-and-pepper hair. 'Coffee?'

'No thanks.'

'What – you don't like the taste of dishwater?' He chuckles at his own joke, tearing open four sugar packs at once, spilling granules all over the place.

She pulls out her second-last cigarette and looks through her pockets. Stupid lighter. Scratch of a match and the short man lights it for her.

'Look, I don't want to put my nose in, but I heard you say you were ... his wife?'

She really looks at him, blowing on his coffee even though she's sure it's been sitting there so long it's lukewarm at best. He won't make eye contact with her, focusing on her left shoulder, her forehead, something past her. Wiry – too skinny to be a cop, she thinks.

'Did you see ... ?'

He nods, a rapid-fire jiggle of his chin that seems to go on and on. 'I brought him in – me and my partner.'

'Can you take me to see him?'

Clears his throat, then clears it again. 'No.'

'Please, I have to – please.'

'Look, it's not that I don't want to, it's just ... ' He looks back down the hall. 'Okay, you can't say anything about this – they don't want it getting out yet, but ... ' His voice lowering to a hiss. 'The body's gone.'

'Gone ... '

'Yeah.'

'Where did it go?'

'Uh, we're not sure. Somebody may have stolen it. Or ... '

'Or what?'

'They've got people on it – it's only a matter of time.'

'So I should just wait?'

'Uh, yeah ... yeah.'

'Thanks.' And she goes quickly this time, a quick break to the doors, back home to get ready for work, waiting tables, waiting for the shift to end, waiting in bed for the sound of the door opening, waiting to hear her son come in, or waiting not to hear anything.

'Wait.'

She turns. The short cop jabs behind him with his thumb. 'I just gotta grab my keys.'

The screech of metal and the back doors of the van come open. The cop steps back for Martha, but there's nothing for her to see. He points. 'He was right there.'

'Show me.'

He looks around the lot nervously, like he's forgotten he's a police officer. 'Look, I'm in a lotta shit as it is.'

'Please.'

He sighs and grunts his way into the back of the van. He offers a hand, but Martha's ditched her cigarette and is already scrabbling in after him. He goes to the small slot that looks into the cab and picks at it, checking something, then comes back. He crouches and puts his hand on the floor, looks up at Martha.

'Go on.'

He plops on his ass and then slowly lies back, stretching out, squirming a little to one side to make sure he's in the right place. With him all laid out like that, Martha can see a dark stain underneath his head. And they don't move and they don't say anything for a while.

So she's there staring down at the cop's face, his eyes fixed past her on the ceiling, her trying to picture this being Van, lying there, naked and dead. His ears sticking out with that goofy grin he took to the grave and all that hair, like some kind of big monkey, the monkey on the placemat. Year of the monkey. The year she was born, the year Slim was born, the year Van left. These markers in her life, divided by a rhythm, every *tick* bringing some new disaster. The next *tick* the end of the world maybe, and her waiting around for it. Van'll come back kickin through the screen door, *I got that milk*, and they'll laugh and they'll all go back to the way it was, exactly the way it was, without the yelling and the name calling and the door slamming and the rest of it. Just the good stuff. Just the roses.

It's the flash of a squad car on its way out that brings Martha around, quickly slipping out of the van, pulling out her pack for her second-last cigarette to find it empty.

'Man, it's really coming down now, eh?' The doors slam closed. They both lean against the side of the van. 'Never would've found him in this. He'd be out there till spring maybe.'

'He never could sit still.'

He does the clearing-his-throat thing again, like the words are hard to bring up. 'What made you think it was him?'

She shrugs because no one really knows anything, least of all about themselves. 'I've gotta get ready for work.'

'Where d'you work?'

She points to Nibblers down the street, orange sign all lit up in bulbs. 'Come by for a coffee sometime. I owe you one.'

'Sure. Maybe later. I've been stuck here all day with this crap.'

'All right then, officer.'

'My name's Wally – Walter.'

'Walter?' She hears her own laugh sneak out on her. 'Then you owe me.'

She pushes away but then his hand is on her arm, warm but shivering with something. 'What was he like?' And he's looking at her, right at her, for the first time. Like what she says could really matter.

'He said nice things.' And she leaves him with that.

At the corner, she looks back. He's still there by the van, all that snow coming down on him, salt-and-pepper hair going white and turning him old.

Maybe she'll stop by Black Cat to pick up another pack. Maybe she won't. She's quitting, tomorrow or one of these days soon. And she'll call someone about that door because look at this snow. She doesn't even bother trying to cover her hair.

8

Normando goes behind the bar at the Sampo, rolling up sleeves to show the blue smear of some tattoo on his forearm. Two lifers are playing a hand of pinochle on a cracked formica tabletop, the leg propped with coasters. Gladys slides into a stool at the bar, accordion oozing across her lap, and Normando places a glass of sherry down which she sips through dentures. The *whisk whisk* of cards, one of the lifers farts and then the hall is dead again under the hum of the beer fridge.

He gets the radio on to drown out all that damned quiet. Some broadcaster coming on about that body everyone'd been gabbing about. A man don't need to be gossiped about when he can't speak up for himself. No respect for the dead. He shuts the damned thing off.

The sound of a door upstairs and Ernie comes clomping down, all bony joints and rumpled clothing. He mumbles something to the card players, who mumble back, and brings his big white beard up to the bar.

'Here early, Norm?'

Normando shrugs and slides a bottle of Northern across. Gladys picks up her drink, moves off to the stage, starts plunking down music stands. Ernie peels pieces off his beer label, tears these into even smaller pieces.

'You heard? Union's talking about another strike. Could be a long one.' He looks up at Normando with quick eyes. 'Gonna be tight times.' Looking away.

'Tight fer who, Ernie?'

'Everyone.'

The doors to the Sampo bang open – figures shuffling in, squinting in the dim light. They come in black vests, scuffed shoes, carrying violins and flutes. Some wave or nod at Normando as they keep shuffling off to the stage.

'Listen, Norm, Sampo's been sold – the Ukrainians.'

Normando looks down at his hands, spread on the stained surface of the bar – thumb missing a tip, couple of fingers bent, calluses slowly peeling away to something pink. Wedding band on one hand, twenty-five-year ring on the other – company logo etched and fading. He picks up a cloth and starts wiping, just to have something to do.

'Gonna take the bar out, turn this place into some kinda daycare or something. Maybe I can get you some work as caretaker – cleaning up – you want.'

The unhappy sound of instruments tuning, some kind of march or dirge, as the folk ensemble warms up.

'Well, anyway, you got the popcorn cart, right? Not like you need two jobs, right?'

So what if he's only been working a coupla evenings a week. They know him here. It's his place. It's not about the damned job. But he doesn't say it.

Ernie drags a crumb out of his beard. 'You hear about Ristimaki? He's got it in the other lung now too.'

Normando keeps on wiping the same spot, a stain that'll never come out. Ristimaki, the poor damned sap.

9

The third punch breaks his nose and the next time Gordon Uranium opens his eyes he's lying on a mountain of garbage behind May's. His shirt is a constellation of blood and somebody has taken his snakeskin boots.

It's just starting to snow, the first lazy flakes of the year. He staggers down the alley, easing his bare feet around broken glass and the liquid gifts of someone's hangover, and out onto Elgin. He squints in the grey November light. Fuck it's cold.

Nursing a beer at the Nickel Bin, Gordon gets to thinking about those damn boots. The same pattern Bronson wore in *Once Upon a Time in the West* – twelve-inch shaft, quarter-inch heel, J-toe and crested with a double rose scallop. Only had them two weeks. Custom-made by the old Serbian widow down in the Donovan, pecking away with arthritic fingers. She offered fresh-fried *krofne* and he supplied the snakeskin – eastern diamondback rattlesnake. Her kitchen smelled like cinnamon and yeast.

'You're bleeding all over my bar.' Foisey, curly hair jammed up under a net, glares at him from behind the register. Gordon tears two strips off a napkin, rolling them between fingertips, and stuffs one capsule up either nostril. He uses the rest of the napkin to mop up the blood on the cracked wooden surface. Nobody else in the place except McGowan, passed out by the pinball table already. Some news report is playing on the set above the beer fridge, the reporter looking all-important holding his microphone. Something about a body gone missing.

'You know who was just in here?' Foisey talking quick, trying to play it cool, but Gordon can smell the nerves. 'Jyrki fuckin Myllarinen.'

He searches but can't find a face for the name. The reporter keeps on going, standing outside the back of a police van. Something nagging Gordon about it, the whole thing making him feel queer, like this whole news report, a body all laid out and cold, is some movie he's already seen.

'Thought he was in Kingston Pen. Fuckin butcher.' Foisey following Gordon's eyes up to the television. The report turning over to the Wolves' latest loss. 'New uniforms, same fuckin shit.' He slaps a dishrag down in front of Gordon and leans over the bar. 'That Lalonde kid's the only good egg in the whole batch, eh?'

Gordon pushes his beer away, half-finished. Coming down on the wing. One, two, three strides. White noise in his ears – the crowd. Then crash. Then nothing.

'Sorry, forgot you don't talk hockey. They just ain't been no good. Not since, y'know, you, well … ' Foisey trails off, getting awkard. He whisks the bottle away under the bar. 'So who rearranged your face?'

Gordon shrugs. Walking home from the bar last night, cutting into the tunnel under the tracks to get out of the rain – a flash, a detonation in his brain – then hitting pavement so hard his head should've popped off. Being dragged, rain freezing to slick. The smell of garbage.

But there's something dangling back there. Just as he climbed the last step down into the underpass. Reflection in a puddle. Gold watch.

'You don't care, I don't care – fuck it.' Foisey wanders off to change the channel. 'Two-fifty for the beer.'

Searching pockets on his torn work jacket. Nothing. Took the wallet too. Gordon shifts on his seat, bare feet rasping against the metal rim of the stool, and clears his throat.

'Okay. Add it to your tab. Y'know, fuck it, heard about Katie – this one's on me.'

Gordon gives Foisey a nod and slides off the stool. Padding across cement toward the door and pushing it open to head back out into the snow.

'What the fuck happened to your boots, man?' McGowan squinting bloodshot in the corner, as the door swings closed.

Standing on the red brick sidewalk outside the Nickel Bin, facing the tracks and train burping ash smoke into steel sky, Gordon thinks about the things he has lost – a long list ending with two boots. He tries to let it go. Watching the engineer, black-capped, swing into the Budd car – glacial steel surface. The car shunting. He tries to let it go. The brakes squeal and then – *crash!* – the cars impacting as the train reverses.

Crash. Shaking something loose in his brain. *Crash* – his nose bursting. *Crash* – the feeling of knuckles on bone. Make sure the gloves come off. Grab with your left, cock the right. You wanna get a good one right there on the cheekbone, leave a shiner. Tattoo the fucker so everyone knows you got him. *Crash* – laying in with the shoulder. *Crash* – the sound of a body hitting the ice. The years crashing together.

'Hey, Killer, somebody think you're too pretty or something?'

Martha walking down Elgin with a cigarette hanging between lipstick. He tries to smile, he'd like her to see him smile, but it hurts. She comes to stand at his shoulder and they both watch as the train shudders out of the station, smeared brick of row housing coming unhidden on the other side of the tracks.

'Listen – I heard. I'm real sorry about Katie,' she says while he tries to let it go. 'Know how attached you were to her.' Seeing red, he tries to let it go. 'You okay?' He tries –

Ah, hell.

Door to the Nickel Bin bangs open, Foisey peering out like an albino from a cave, tossing something. 'It's fuckin November, Gordo. Jee-sus!' Pink slippers hitting the sidewalk next to Gordon. 'Lost-and-found box – somebody mighta puked on them. I dunno.' Door banging closed.

He sits on the curb, bare feet in gutter and leaves. She bends and grabs a slipper, waiting for him. 'Your colour, I think.' He slides his foot in – too tight. She looks right at him – eyes like rum, a network of lines sneaking in, and her face too warm for this day. Her smile flattens out. She pulls something small and hard from between his toes. 'Oh, shit.'

A station wagon screeches up, front tire jumping the curb and banging down. 'Fuck's sake, Martha!' A woman with an ugly thatch of purple hair hops out of the car and walks toward them, chewing gum like it's a profession. Martha groans and stubs her cigarette out in the concrete planter.

'You fuckin left me with the tab at the Empress!'

'I didn't have anythi– '

'And I had to finish your goddamn beer.' The woman stops in front of them. She looks at Gordon and blinks. 'Hey. You're the hockey pla– '

'Shut up, Lucy.'

'Viper – no, Cobra.' She giggles. 'Why're you wearing slippers?'

'Lucy.'

'What?' She looks at Martha's hand, the thing she pulled from his toes still pinched between finger and thumb. 'Whatcha got?'

Martha balls her hand into a fist. 'Nothi– '

Lucy snatches at her, giggling like it's some kind of game, one that's fun only to her. Gordon gives her a little nudge and she falls on her ass in the planter. 'Fuck's sake, you two – I was just jokin!'

She reaches out, hands snapping open and closed. 'Now help me up.'

He pulls her to her feet and turns to Martha. She's looking at him. Like he's naked. Not in an I-want-to-fuck-you way, but like she knows him. And she probably does. All the bad shit, and still she looks.

'Hey!' Lucy holding up the small, shiny thing she took from Martha. 'This's just like those boots at the restaurant.'

'Lucy!'

'What?'

Gordon grabs it from her and turns.

'Hey!'

'Gordon – stop!'

But he's halfway down Durham before he finally opens his clenched fist – the glossy shine of a snake scale, like a beacon. Martha's voice coming after, 'Don't hurt him, Gordon, don't hurt him!'

Oswald's Pawnshop is in the Flour Mill. Walking past lines buckling with laundry, old Italian women beating their linen with brooms, the abandoned silos hanging over it all. Gordon remembers he always hated the Flour Mill.

It was just a little farther up, at that place behind the go-kart track, where he bought that diamondback rattler seven years back. He remembers it cold and motionless behind the glass, and him recognizing something there. Bringing it back to his apartment – the space almost empty except for her terrarium. Seven years of coming home to something. Giving her dinner, making his own. And then one day, nothing.

He stops, slippers deep in slush, at the door to Oz's shithole. Peering in through the glass to see the counter empty, he cracks the door – remembering to reach up to stop the bell before pushing the rest of the way through.

Shelves lined with dust and junk, yellowed price tags dangling in the fluorescent buzz. He pads across linoleum and vaults over the counter, following a short hallway to the swinging light bulb of a stockroom. With his broad back to the doorway, Oz is bent over a box, humming to himself in the half-light.

Gordon grabs Oz by the wrist, torquing his elbow and pinning the big man against the cold cement of the wall.

'Hey!' A short jab to the kidney takes the fight out of him, and Gordon spins Oz around, now jamming his left forearm under the other man's big, drooping chin.

'Gordo.' He's gasping, wheezing, walrus moustache quivering. 'What the fuck? Lemme go, I didn't do anything – I swear.'

Gordon presses in a little tighter to watch the fat man's eyes bulge. Pin him up against the boards. It's in your end – pressure's on. Scuffle for the puck, kick it out, get it back on your stick. It's all on you. Dump it. The crowd – fuck, the crowd.

'Gordo!' Oz sputters, going purple, and he finally eases off, stepping back as the big man slides down the wall. 'The hell's your problem? You want me to get the cops down here on you? Chrissakes.' Rubbing at his throat, Oz dips his eyes to take in Gordon's slippers. 'The boots – why didn't you just say so?'

Back in the front room, Oz passes him a yellow square of paper over the counter – chicken scratches. 'Didn't buy those boots, something off about that kid, but I got the addy for the other stuff he brought in. Fake, likely.' Oz eyes him, turning something over in his big skull, and sighs. 'Listen – I seen that kid before. Think he squats up in one of those tailing shacks behind the Gatch.'

Gordon nods and walks to the door. Gatchell – one step farther down the ladder. He gets a hand on the doorknob and turns.

'Damn shame about Katie,' Oz says. 'Maybe you should get yourself another one.' Door swinging open, bell jingling, and Oz's voice chases him out onto the street. 'It's just a pair of boots, Gordo.'

It's a long walk to Gatchell, and with each step Gordon's mind slips a little further back on itself. Just a pair of boots. Step step. Just boots. Step step. Just. Step. Boots. Step.Boots.Step.Bootsstep.

Katie.

He stumbles, and somebody yells at him, and he turns, ready to fight. You get a skate caught in bad ice and they'll come after you when they see you weak. But it's just some chubby kid waving his slipper at him. Some kid like a whole bunch of other kids. *Hey! Can you sign this? Please. You're gonna be something. You're gonna be something big. The next one.*

He takes the slipper and leaves the kid behind, with all that hope in his eyes. He just can't bear it. He keeps on down Elgin, the slippers soaked. But he ignores it. Keep your eyes on the puck. You dump it, but it's picked off centre ice. You square up, watch him bring it over the line. He's got his head down, charging, as you sneak up on his side. Score tied, thirty seconds left. You lower the shoulder, one two three strides.

Each step brings him closer to Gatchell. Closer to just putting this whole thing behind him.

He remembers the day he brought the rattler in to that old Serb down in the Donovan. Gordon had been careful with her, careful not to bring his hand near for the first few hours, knowing the heat of his touch would trigger the hidden electricity in her jaw – venom and fang. He brought her wrapped in newspaper, finally stiff, to that baba – white drifts of hair coiled in a bun. He watched the woman temper the leather, work the cork and finally peel the rattlesnake's skin back, leaving only the black marbles of the eyes behind. She had been kind enough to ignore him each time he cleared his throat, swallowing back the image of his own skin stripped away – laying open the black core of loneliness inside.

Gordon stands before the slag banks, the lights of Gatchell at his back. He stands, one foot in slipper and on asphalt, the other bare and on the grit of slag.

He leaves the city behind and walks into the narrow path. On either side, the banks, heaps of black pebbles, tower over him. The banks seem to run straight to the horizon, and he scans for some break, some hint of the cluster of abandoned shacks the foreman grafted into the hillside. They still run the slag dumps at night. People used to come watch the rail cars pour the melted waste down the sides of the hills, a spreading wasteland. Some would sneak a trunk-load home for the driveway. But the novelty of it is gone. The only people who come up here now are crazies, junkies or people with something to hide.

There. A movement – shuffling – somebody walking toward him. Gordon veers to the right, sticking to the shadow of the bank of slag, and waits.

A tuneless whistling slices through the cold air, and the figure comes clear as it draws closer. A man. A young man. Peach fuzz. Can't be much older than nineteen. T-shirt, even in this cold. Some tough case. And as the kid passes him, Gordon catches the shine of gold at the wrist. A watch.

The kid's crossing into their zone and he angles up along the boards, sneaking up on the right side. The kid's skating fast, but his head's still down. He cuts in on him, coming up hard, and lays in with the shoulder. *Wham!* – and they both get tangled and hit the ice.

They're on the slag and the kid thrashes, catching Gordon with the familiar sensation of a right hook, and he loses his hold, the kid leaping to his feet and rushing for the opposite bank. Gordon drags his ass off the ground, kicks off the remaining slipper and gives chase.

The kid scampers cat-like up the bank – loosing an avalanche of slag down on him. The kid clambers to the top and stands on the crest of the ridge, turning to look down at him. A kick from above, a cloud of dust and rock, and Gordon sees it. The network of the diamondback pattern on the kid's feet. A glimpse and he's out of sight over the ridge.

The furnace in his gut propels Gordon to the top of the bank. Behind him, he can see the steady snowfall peppering the lake of slag and beyond, all the lights in the mining town winking on. Turning back, he can see the dark shapes of the shacks huddling on the side of the bank below. Only one light, the flicker of a lantern, in a window. Door slam – the light goes out.

Gordon, with his eyes focused on this shack – eyes on the puck – descends. His feet leaving a trail of blood on the snow and slag in his wake.

Gordon moves between the cindered and rotting wood of the buildings. The smell of decay reaching past the paper still lodged in his nostrils. He finds the shack, camouflaged by the rest, but through the window he can see the shape of a mattress and a lantern, ember still fading, hanging on a nail. No one in sight.

Gordon circles the structure, settling in front of the only door. He raises a foot to kick, but spotting the mess attached to his ankle, he lays in with his shoulder instead. The lock splinters and Gordon pours into the dark interior.

Another fist connects with his jaw. And the kid is up and skating away, carrying the puck deep into their zone. He sees the number on the back of the kid's sweater – #18. Draft pick with the North Stars. Hotshot. Twenty seconds left. If he scores now, it's done. He pulls himself to his feet and gives chase. The kid's fast, but Gordon wants it more. Fifteen seconds. No one else around. All on him. Send it to overtime. Give them one last chance. The kid shifts the puck to his left side. He's gonna go backhand. A flash move. He can see it happening, down low under the pads. The playoffs over just like that. Everything over. Ten seconds. The white noise of the crowd. Scouts watching. *Crash* – people pounding the glass shouting. *Crash* – you're gonna be big – the next one! *Crash* – hit em, hit em, Python! *Crash* – Hit em, Killer! The puck is cocked, he's not gonna reach him. Five seconds. He drops his stick, reaches out with his left, grabbing the back of the kid's jersey, pulls him in. *Crash* – kill em! Kill em, Gordo! *Crash* – his fist hits the back of the kid's skull. *Crash.* The kid hits the ice, head bouncing. *Crash.* The arena is silent. He doesn't see the puck. He doesn't see anything. Everything crashes down.

Gordon feels nothing again. No fire, no cold, just nothing. He tosses the kid on the mattress and stands over him. The kid doesn't move.

A slow glow fills the cabin, orange fire, revealing everything in stark detail. Corncob-yellow paint has disguised the rotting wood, fading photographs smiling from behind tacks, a small collection of tinned food, and at the heart of it all – snake scales and a gold watch. He glances out the window. The carts have pulled up on the embankment across from the shack, puking up a stream of molten slag, glowing in the night.

He looks down at this kid, maybe not even nineteen. Still not moving. The body on the television. The body on the ice. This body here. His body on his bed in his empty apartment. His snake laid out in her terrarium. They all look the same.

The kid groans. 'Please. Don't kill me.'

Gordon feels all his breath go out and he sinks to his knees, weak – so weak. He leans over the kid and reaches out to brush his hair, wipe off some of the blood, but the kid rolls away. Looking at the small body on this mattress, he can see some kind of vice already closing in, and he thinks about his own place, his one-room bachelor above the newsstand. And he wants to tell him, I won't hurt you. There's more in this world than all this shit, this slag. He wants to save him. Just kick the puck away.

But instead he reaches out again and drags the boots off the kid's feet. He pulls them on, his own feet sticky with blood, catching the vapour of warmth inside. He stands again, leather creaking, the sensation flooding back – his first day wearing them, two weeks ago. Walking back from the Donovan, feeling the warmth, the comfort of having something he cared for so close. Taking the edge off everything so cold creeping in at all corners. And he imagines he can feel, at the left ankle, the place where he scratched the name. Five letters and a number.

'Hey.' The kid, now sitting up, holds something out to him – the gold watch. 'Take it. My old man gave it to me. It's all I got.'

Gordon feels something stick in his throat. Just boots. Just a snake. Just a name. Nothing's just anything. Dead inside and out, they all look the same. They're all the same. And they all have the same name. Katie #18.

He pushes the kid's hand back and tries to smile, but it hurts. He turns and heads back out, trying not to look at the kid – the blood from his nose matching Gordon's own. He shuts the door as softly as he can and walks off, the cooling slag closing the night in around him. You can't save anyone. Not even yourself.

It's only when he climbs the stairs to his room, key in lock, that he remembers the wallet he forgot, the five maybe ten dollars inside.

Hell, let him have something. Pushing through to the roar of the empty space beyond.

10

Normando is sinking into the flowered chesterfield, sucking on a bowl of stewed prunes, the television strobe lighting up the room. Randolph Scott is coming through a canyon, white cowboy hat pushed back as he speeches at Joel McCrea about poor men. McCrea's cradling a rifle like a baby and he looks off into the great blue yonder and Normando pulls himself out of the swamp of the chesterfield, dialling the volume up until the speakers rattle so he can hear this. Hear him say it. Almost chokes on a prune straining to hear it.

'All I want is to enter my house justified.'

Pat steps in front of the set.

'Norm – Norm, can you turn that down? Turn it down, Norm.' She doesn't wait, yanking the plug out. 'Need you to come look at my pee, Norm – it's got a funny colour. Can you come look at my pee, Norm?'

Normando struggles out of the chesterfield, making the move to plug the set back in.

'You've already seen that one, Norm. Can you just take a blue minute here and look at my pee?'

'Pat, I don't need to see yer goddamned pee.'

'Well, you just go ahead and write that on my gravestone, Norm.' Pat turning away, turning back. 'What're you doing moping about in here with the lights out?'

'Lights weren't out – watching the TV.'

'Always moping about, you. You just haven't been the same, Norm. No sir.' She lets the words hang, incomplete, her face all pinched up as she walks out of the room. *Not since you retired* – but she doesn't say it, and her not saying it lets the words become something else. Something that reaches back farther. Not since the mine. Not since the boy. Not since ever.

She chirps up again from the other room. 'You hear bout that boy they found out on the highway?'

'Yep.'

‘What d’you think about that then?’

And he doesn’t answer, because you don’t talk about the damned dead. They’re gone and that’s that. Let em have their peace.

‘This came for you today – first one.’ Scurrying back in, she shoves an envelope into his hand – plastic crinkle of a government window and his name typed in. ‘You’re an old man now.’

She leaves him alone to fumble with the plug, to curse, to sit back and be silent in the dark of the living room.

11

Emilia first mentions something about a body after they crawl under the wooden fort. The *thump thump* of the other kids running around above them, laughing like a bunch of dorks. Emilia Zanetti and Elwy Zott side by side down here in the dark with their plastic ninjas and the last of the earwigs.

'And my dad said they don't even know his *name*, isn't that nuts?' Emilia always asking her questions twice. 'Isn't it?' But she never really needs an answer, so Elwy doesn't say anything. Instead he tries to whistle. Because he's nervous. And he can make great whistling faces but he can't make great whistling sounds. Or any whistling sounds. It's what Emilia calls his ghost whistle. Under the fort, Elwy purses his lips and makes strange breathing noises.

'Quit ghost whistling, El, this is serious.'

Elwy stops making strange breathing noises and concentrates on not being nervous. It's hard because thinking about dead bodies is the number one thing that makes him nervous. That and having to write on the board in class.

'And my dad said it was definitely murder.'

Elwy shuts his eyes tight so that murder can't get into them. Emilia's dad is an expert of everything. Because he reads the paper every morning and watches TV every night and you aren't allowed to talk to him when he does these things because they are more important.

Emilia and Elwy side by side in class, both raising their hands in succession, Zanetti and then Zott, the same way it's been since Grade 3 when Elwy's dad had his heart exploded and he and his mom moved into that brownstone across the street from the school. There was that bit in Grade 5 when Andrew Zimmerman split them up, but nobody talked to him because he wore jogging pants and anyway he got held back a year. Not for wearing jogging pants but for being dumb.

Mr. Bedard and his big shiny head are up at the board, trying to teach them something boring about music theory. Elwy's book is open on his desk, him doodling in the margins.

'And my dad said there was blood everywhere, all over the back of the van, the walls, the floor, the ceiling. Everywhere.'

Doug Degault with his big eavesdropping ears one seat up and to the left. 'Emilia, your dad cleans the fuckin urinals.'

'Kiss my grapefruit, celery lips.' Emilia leans in closer to Elwy, whispering so Doug can't hear. 'And you know what else my dad said this morning? Know what else?'

But then Allie at the front is pointing outside and saying something to Mr. Bedard and then chairs are sliding back and everyone's moving to the windows. Everyone except Emilia, still chirping behind him as Elwy goes to press his face to the glass. 'When they opened the doors there was all that blood and that was it.' Snowflakes coming down, hitting the brown grass. These first ones'll melt, sure, but it won't be long before they'll pile up and Elwy's already thinking about his black GT Racer in the basement, the hill down at the park, all the snowball fights, the skating rink down at Queen's, the icicles on the side of his house, the sound of the plough going by while you're lying in bed thinking about all that stuff.

Then Emilia's beside him, tugging at his sleeve. 'You hear me? There was all that blood but no body. That dead guy just disappeared.' Elwy's breath on the glass, everything crusting over.

After the bell and everyone is gone, except Elwy sharpening all his pencils, three of them, like he does every day. The warm smell of pencil shavings in his hands as he walks to the front and drops them in the brown trash can. Mr. Bedard peering down at sheet music spread out on his desktop. 'See you tomorrow, Elwy.'

Elwy nods and goes for the door and then comes back to stand at the edge of the desk, picking at the corner where the wood has splintered. Mr. Bedard looks up with droopy eyes over his droopy moustache. 'Working on your whistle?'

Elwy shakes his head and peels a really nice flake of wood off the desk. 'Mr. Bedard?'

'Mm?'

'Do some people live forever?'

'What?'

'Do some people, like some people, never die?'

'Uh. Hm.' Shuffling his papers and touching his moustache. 'Well, Elwy, some people can live a long, long time. But not forever, no.'

'Oh.' Elwy starts to pick his nose and then remembers it's rude. 'Even He-Man and Dracula?'

'Everybody's got a time, Elwy.'

'Oh.' Mr. Bedard goes back to his sheet music. Elwy plays with the hem of his shirt. 'Mr. Bedard?'

'Yes, Elwy?'

'Can people, like some people, come back after they're dead? Like once in a while?'

Mr. Bedard leans back from his desk and stares very hard at Elwy. It's that look his mom gives him when he coughs funny and she thinks he's getting the epidemic. 'You've got lots of time, Elwy. Lots and lots.' Mr. Bedard making a smile like he's trying to reassure one of them.

Elwy sliding through the slush on the roadside, his feet already soaked, feeling great. Emilia up on the sidewalk, carrying both their bags, not talking for the first time in hours, but thinking hard. Elwy knows this because she always looks angry when she thinks and right now Emilia looks really angry. The snow's still coming down and Elwy can feel the *pff pff* of the flakes as they land in his hair.

Elwy reaches the metal stairs at the end of Marion and waits for Emilia so they can race to the landing. Even though he lives across the street from the school, he walks Emilia partway home because she won't give him his bag until they reach the landing. And also because they're best friends and spending time with your best friend is the number one important thing to Elwy. That and getting up early on Saturday to watch cartoons.

Emilia gets to the bottom of the stairs and shoves Elwy's bag at him. 'There's only one way a body can disappear. Somebody takes it. That's the only way.'

Elwy squirms into his backpack and shrugs. 'What about magic?'

She thinks about this, looking angrier than ever. 'Okay. Two ways.' She starts to climb the stairs, not even trying to race. 'You're coming over to my house to play Commodore.'

In Emilia's bedroom with the rainbow carpet, Elwy plays thirty-two straight rounds of Pitfall. Thirty-two straight rounds without the mention of a body. Emilia lies on her bed the whole time with her enormous cat Brutus on her chest, and when Elwy falls into a crocodile's mouth on his thirty-third round she finally sits up, Brutus oozing off her and pooling on the floor in a mound of fat and orange fur.

'We're going to find the body, El.'

This is a very bad idea, Elwy thinks, but he also knows Emilia won't care that he thinks this. He liked it better when they were playing Commodore and not talking about dead bodies. Talking about dead bodies makes him think about zombie movies which makes him think about zombies. Zombies being the number one thing that scares him.

'Stop ghost whistling. Look, I'll make a thermos of hot chocolate and it'll be like an adventure.'

Elwy stops making strange breathing noises. 'Mom'll have a hairy conniption if I miss dinner.'

'So call and tell her you're sleeping over.'

'What about your dad?'

'He works tonight. Graveyard shift. He won't know. Or care.' Flicking her red hair in a way that says *big deal* but Elwy knows means something else.

'Can I at least go home and get my snowpants, Em?'

Emilia digs in her closet, finally pulling out a pair of fluorescent pink snowpants and tossing them at Elwy. 'We'll start downtown.'

Emilia struggles through the heavy doors of the police station, dragging Elwy behind her. 'Em, this is where the bad people go. Mom says.'

'Magnum PI always goes in guns blazing, so that's what we do too.'

There's a man in uniform at the long, cracked wooden counter, reading a newspaper. Elwy tugs at Emilia's coat. 'Aren't they gonna recognize you, Em?'

She swats him away. 'He never brings me to work, you cornichon.'

He tugs at her coat again. 'What if we get in trouble and they throw us in with all the murderers, Em. I don't wanna be murderered.'

'Elwy Xander,' hissing in her most mom-like scolding voice, making him immediately shut up. He only ever hears his full name when he's done something really, really bad. Police stations feel like libraries. Emilia sticks him in one of the waiting chairs and goes to the counter, standing on her tiptoes and leaning with her elbows.

The police officer on the other side looks down his glasses at all that red frizzy hair and smiles. 'Already bought a box of cookies this week, sweetie.'

'I'd like to inquire about the circumstances surrounding the mysterious disappearance of a body.'

The officer's smile drips away and he pulls off his glasses. 'What?'

'The body that disappeared this morning from these very premises.'

'Not another one. Listen, kid, I've had a long day, okay?'

'Do you have any leads on the whereabouts of the corpse?'

The officer starts to come around the counter. 'I have to lock you up or what?' He stops when he sees Elwy hiding behind Emilia. 'Why's your friend breathing like that?'

'He's whistling.'

In a booth at Nibblers, the diner just down the street, Elwy sips his chocolate milkshake, his number two favourite flavour since they didn't have strawberry, while Emilia taps her fingers on the tabletop, looking angry again.

'So does that mean we can go home, Em?'

'Not yet.'

'But we didn't find anything out and we could still make it for dinner.'

'Not me, I got to make my own.'

Elwy feels bad that Emilia's mom doesn't make her dinner anymore since she left Emilia's dad for the Other Man. 'You could come over. Mom's making chicken fingers tonight. Chicken fingers're my favourite.'

Emilia watches the man hunched over at the counter, the only other customer. Red plaid jacket, lightning-blond beard, rubber boots dripping slush on the floor. Dipping a tea bag in and out of a cup. His eyes dart her way, locking on her, and she feels cold, right down to her toes.

Then he's back on the waitress with the big perm as she comes out of the kitchen. He leans over and says something to her as she passes. She gives him a long hard look and then says something back. The cold man's lip curls, like a dog when it smiles, and he stands. He hisses three words that Emilia can barely hear. 'Where is he?'

The door opens with a jingle and two men walk in, stamping their feet to kick off the slush. One is skinny and dark, the other pale and short. The cold man looks their way, sharp, and then back at the waitress. Pulling a few coins out of his pocket and dumping them on the counter.

'Can we order chicken fingers here at least?'

'Hush up, El.'

The two men make their way across the diner and sit in the next booth. The cold man leaves, the waitress looking down at the money he left like it's dog poop. She pats at her curls, and Emilia can see her hands are shaking.

'With plum sauce.'

'Hush.'

Elwy watches the two men getting settled. Peering from behind his milkshake, he can see a piece of one face. Dark skin, twinkly eyes, big smile at the approaching waitress. She smiles back, but it's fake, plastic like one of his MUSCLE Men figurines. 'The usual?'

'Yeah, but I'll take a Northern, Martha. Been a long couple days.'

'Sure thing, Fish.' Turning to the other man, then smiling, a real one. 'Oh, hey – you came by.'

'You know my partner?'

'Yeah, we met. Dishwater?'

The short man laughs, wiggling all over with it. 'Coffee, yeah.'

Elwy watches the waitress with the big perm walk back to the bar. He sucks up the last of his milkshake and keeps on sucking, rattling at the bottom of his glass. 'So we can go home now, Em?'

'No.'

'But – '

'Hush for the love of rhubarb.'

Elwy sulks, which he does by scrunching up his eyes and blowing air out his nostrils. Elwy sulks a lot. When people don't listen to him, when he gets the answer wrong in class, when his mom makes him stop reading and go to bed, when Emilia won't let him have his turn at Commodore, when –

'I tell you, I'm fuckin exhausted.'

Elwy stops sulking to giggle. Emilia bites her lip and turns purple. She never swears. Her dad said her mom always swore like a sailor, and sailors use all the bad words, so instead of the bad words Emilia uses vegetables. Vegetables don't sound mean when you say them. Elwy wonders if the two men at the next booth are sailors.

'I mean we been up all night freezin our asses off.' It's the twinkly-eye man talking. Elwy likes his twinkly eyes – they look happy even though he doesn't sound happy. 'We drive all the way back here and then they keep us at the station all day so they can ask us the same damn question over and over again. I mean how the hell am I supposed to know where it went? I didn't even want to touch him in the first place. Maybe he got up and walked away.'

Elwy can see the back of the other man's head nodding, nodding being the only thing needed of him. The waitress plunks the drinks in front of the men. The twinkly-eye man smiles at her with one corner of his mouth. 'Hey, Martha, any naked frozen men come in here looking for a cup of coffee? Maybe a burger?'

'No.' She keeps on smiling, but now it's a different kind, like the smile Elwy's mom gave him when she told him about his dad's heart explosion. 'Not today.'

The short man grabs the twinkly-eye man's sleeve and hisses something as the waitress walks off.

'What? Just joking. Hell of a thing. You go to sign us in, I take a piss and when we open it up, nothin.' He drains half his bottle in one gulp. 'I dunno. Maybe we left the van unlocked or something. Maybe somebody was walking by. Maybe … ' He drains the rest. 'I tell ya, they want to find this guy they should dredge up Ramsey. That guy, whatsis name, you remember that guy? Dumped that body out there a few years back. And they found that girl out by Moonlight, just floatin there. That housewife too, husband dropped her in the crick. Almost all water runs down to Ramsey, underground or whatever. Maybe he'll end up there too. They should dredge it before it starts to freeze up. Hell of a thing.'

Elwy is down at Ramsey Lake almost every day in the summer. His mom sits in a beach chair and reads while he and Emilia swim at the beach down by the amphitheatre. Elwy pictures zombies floating in the water, hair brushing up against him like the slimy weeds he hates.

'C'mon.' Emilia out of the booth and zipping up his jacket for him, helping to pull on his mitts.

'We going home?'

'Nope.' Toque down over his eyes so he has to tilt his head back to see. 'We're going to the lake.'

'But it's too cold to swim and what about the zombies?'

'C'mon.' Dragging him by the hand to the door, the waitress giving them one last big fake grin like her big fake hair and back at the booth the twinkly-eye man says it again, 'Hell of a thing,' like it's the worst curse of all.

At the mouth of the underpass, Elwy plops down on the top step, puts on his best sulk and refuses to budge no matter how many vegetables Emilia cusses at him. He waits until she runs out of vegetables and has started into fruits and nuts.

'Why do we got to find it?'

'Because.'

'Because why?'

'Just because, you cashew.'

'Because is not a reason.'

'Because maybe there's a reward or something or maybe they'll put us on the news at 6 p.m. My dad always watches the news at 6 p.m.'

'But I don't wanna find it.'

'Quit being such a baby.'

'I'm not a baby.'

'Yes you are. So go home, you big baby, I'll find it on my own.'

'Don't call me a baby.'

'Baby baby baby.'

'But you're not supposed to go to the lake alone because you can't swim.'

'I'm not swimming – it's snowing out, you stupid flaxseed.'

Emilia stomps down the stairs and turns the corner into the tunnel. Elwy waits, his bum getting cold, no longer sulking because there's no one to see. The scuffle of feet on sidewalk and Elwy turns to find a man passing by, big shoulders stooped in a stained green work jacket like the one Emilia's dad wears. His nose is all black and red and there's tissue coming out of his nostrils. He trips, loses something – a shoe – but keeps on walking.

'Hey!' Elwy grabbing the shoe, a slipper, and chasing after. 'Hey!' He catches up to the tissue-nose man, him loping even with just one slipper and Elwy running along beside him shaking the slipper in the tissue-nose man's face. 'Hey.'

The tissue-nose man stops, looks at the slipper like Elwy's mom looked at him that time he pooped in the tub by accident. Elwy's not sure if he's made the tissue-nose man mad and for a minute he thinks he's going to get yelled at. Getting yelled at's the number one thing that makes Elwy cry and he feels his eyes itching just thinking about it. But the tissue-nose man doesn't yell. He takes the slipper and puts it back on his foot. And stands there. Elwy thinks he's going to ask the where're-your-parents question, but he doesn't. He just stands and stares. Elwy tries to whistle and thinks about walking away but walking away without saying something would be rude, like not giving grandma a kiss before you leave even though her face tastes like makeup.

Then it hits him. 'Whoa.' The tissue-nose man's face on a card in Emilia's dad's album. 'You're like Wayne Gretzky, aren't you?'

The tissue-nose man gets a look, his eyes all scrunched up, and his top lip rolls up to show his teeth, but it's not a smile. He's said something bad. Like when Grandma threatens him with the wooden spoon bad. This guy doesn't like Wayne Gretzky. He doesn't think he's Great or anything. Elwy's never been hit before, except by Emilia, but that doesn't count because she wasn't an adult, but if he was ever gonna be hit it'd be now.

Then he sees he's wrong. Wayne Gretzky makes the tissue-nose man sad. Really, really sad. Like when his mom talks about his dad sad.

'My dad died.' He doesn't know why he's said it. Maybe because it's the most honest thing in the world he can think of. 'His heart exploded.' The tissue-nose man doesn't say anything, he just keeps staring, and Elwy thinks he might be staring at his pink snowpants. 'They're not mine, they're Emilia's.' The tissue-nose man doesn't say anything again. 'She can't swim and if she falls in she might drown.' The tissue-nose man still doesn't say anything. 'I should go. I don't want her to die, dying is no good for anything.'

But there's still only staring and it hits Elwy – the grey face, bags under the eyes, the red stuff running from his nose to his mouth. A zombie. Right here, right out of the movies. First there'd be groaning and then cold fingers reaching and then *crunch crunch* go his brains. All he can do is close his eyes and plug his ears and blow through his lips.

When he opens his eyes, the tissue-nose man is walking off down the street. Just like that. Not a zombie – still alive. Like he'd been paused like a movie at a good part when you go pee and when you get back you hit play again and it keeps going like you never went pee or anything.

Before the tissue-nose man turns the corner, he kicks the slipper off again, and Elwy notices for the first time. They're pink. Just like his snowpants.

Then he hears a *squeaksqueak* and a cart rolls around the corner, a shadowy thing pushing it, and Elwy yells for Emilia, chasing her into the tunnel.

He catches up to her on the hillside over the park. The lake asleep, snow disappearing into it like it never mattered to anybody. 'I'm sorry for calling you a baby,' she says.

All the trees big and black against all that collecting white. Elwy doesn't like trees at night because they look like giants. 'Can I have some hot chocolate now?'

'No.'

The padlock on the canoe club's gone frosty, but Emilia holds it in between her hands and blows into it for a bit. This time the key turns. Emilia has copies of all her dad's keys. She learned by the fifth time he passed out in the car and she found him in the garage the next morning. She had to break the window with a fry pan to wake him up for work.

They slip into the old wooden shack, Emilia pulling the cord on the light bulb, throwing shadows all over the place.

Elwy only has to whine a little bit to get Emilia to put her life jacket on, her little head poking out of all that orange like a Ring Pop, and within fifteen minutes they're in the water. Emilia in the back steering, of course.

She takes them out away from the canoe club and with every few strokes Elwy looks over his shoulder at the shack getting smaller and smaller on the shore. Now a grey dot, now a grey speck, now a grey gone.

'Where're we going, Em?'

'To the deepest part of the lake.'

'Why?'

'Cause that's where the underwater currents are, that's where it'll come out.'

'But how'll we find it if it's on the bottom?'

'Dead bodies float in cold water, El. Everybody knows that.'

Elwy remembers a movie his mom didn't know he watched late one night about underwater Nazi zombies. Zombies can live underwater because they don't breathe. Zombies could be anywhere.

'Stop ghost whistling and paddle. You're making us go in circles.'

Elwy paddles a couple more times, grunting with each stroke, and looks around. The snow is drawn in like a curtain and he can't see the shore in any direction. It's like being in the middle of one of those snow globes in that box in the basement labelled *Christmas*. That box that Elwy and his dad used to open every December first. That box was all closed up and double taped like the coffin at the funeral all closed up because Elwy's mom said no one wants to look at somebody like that. It was like going up to stare in the windows of a house when nobody's home. Nothing to see but a whole lot of empty.

'You ever seen a dead body before, Em?'

'Brutus brought a busted-up chipmunk in through my window once. It just lay there breathing for a while and then it died.'

'What'd it look like?'

'Like a chipmunk.'

'No, what'd it look like when it was dead?'

'It didn't look like anything.'

Something comes toward them, or they're coming toward something, big and even darker than all the darkness around them. It's a body, for sure, Elwy can make out the head and the feet. It's the body of a giant, like those trees in the park, a sleeping giant with a mouth open and hungry. Some little noise comes running up his throat and then Emilia behind him says, 'Elwy, watch out, we're gonna hit that island.'

His heart inching its way back inside him while he pushes up against the rock with his paddle, slowing them down. They paddle around the shore to a low point and Emilia steers them, grinding, up on the sand. 'Here.'

Out of the canoe, they climb on hands and knees up a hump of rock, Elwy landing in a heap at the top, panting little clouds. It's a small island with a couple of trees and it doesn't look like a giant at all, it's more like a turtle. They're on the mound of the shell and it slopes down to a long, low neck.

'You see anything?' Emilia standing beside him with one hand over her eyes, scanning the water like those pictures of pirate captains looking for booty. '*Any*thing?'

Elwy sees rock, a few trees and lots and lots of water.

'No, you radish, like a body.'

'Can we have the hot chocolate now, Em?'

'In a bit. Let's look around some more.'

'Why here?' Elwy throws a rock in the water. 'It's just a stupid island.'

'It's a good home base. You can see all over. We'll be able to spot it when it surfaces.'

'What if it doesn't?'

'It will.'

'Then what?'

'Then we'll bring it back and everything's gonna be great, you'll see.'

Elwy follows Emilia down the rocky mound. They push through a couple of birch trees and climb out along the neck of the turtle, standing on its head. There are names spray-painted and scratched all over the rocks here. Many boys and girls loving many other boys and girls forever. Elwy wonders how you can love forever if you can't live forever.

They crawl on their stomachs to the edge where someone has sprayed *diving rock* in big letters, and right below that *enter the void* and right below that *Slim loves Francie*. They peer over the edge into the black water. Elwy thinks about the chicken fingers and plum sauce he didn't have.

'Can we please have the hot chocolate now?'

'Not yet.'

'Why and don't just say because.'

'Because.' Emilia rolls on her side to look at him. 'There isn't any.'

'But you promised.'

'I didn't promise.'

'Saying is promising.'

'There was none in the cupboard, okay? We ran out. Dad said it's not an *essential*.'

'I'm tired and cold and hungry for chicken fingers and I need to pee and my mom's gonna kill me if we ever get home and I didn't even get any hot chocolate and you promised.' Elwy rolls onto his back with a big huff. 'We're never gonna find this stupid body.'

'Don't say that.'

'Well, we won't.'

'But I got to.'

He turns his head to look at her. 'There isn't any stupid reward anyway, so why do we gotta find it?'

'I just got to.'

'Is it because your mom doesn't make you dinner anymore because she left with the Other Man or because your dad doesn't love you?'

Emilia's face gets all scrunched up like he's just been really mean, the meanest ever, and Elwy didn't mean to be mean, he was only asking. She doesn't say anything, just gives him that look and then rolls away, her back moving in and out with her breath. Emilia doesn't cry, but if she did cry she'd be crying right now. Elwy wants to stop her back from moving in and out so much, but he doesn't know what to say or do.

He doesn't know if she's hurt or mad, but if she's mad she might not talk to him ever again. They'll sit next to each other in class but she'll pretend like he doesn't even exist, like she did that one day when he pushed her into a snowbank, except now it'll be forever and he won't get to walk her to the metal stairs and he won't go over to play Commodore anymore. All of his number one favourite things gone like that. And it's just so awful that Elwy cries for both of them, having to be so alone. And when he's done crying he stares at Emilia's back, which has stopped moving in and out so much, and he thinks about all the forevers he has ever known.

'Why do people got to die, Em?'

And for a second he's so sure she'll have the answer. She'll be able to tell him. But she can't because she's snoring.

Elwy rolls onto his tummy and stares into the water. His reflection lying there on top, Elwy with his favourite toque and his wet teary face. He leans down close to stare into his mirror eyes. There's something white there, a white dot in his left eyeball. A speck growing larger, expanding in his eye, filling it, oozing across his cheek.

Then he realizes it's something past his reflection, something rising from down deep.

It rises slowly, taking shape as it gets closer. A body, so white it almost glows like the stars on Elwy's bedroom ceiling. A naked man. His hands stretching above him, reaching.

Zombies. He thinks about zombies in old black and white films and the teeth and the biting and the blood but he can't move. Dad, he thinks about Dad and the coffin all closed up and Dad white and naked like this inside, white and naked in the water. Me, he thinks about himself lying in the water, so cold and so alone and nobody looking for him.

But it's not him or Dad or any zombie, it's a man. He can't make out the face because the hair is waving back and forth in the water, dark like seaweed.

A man rising from the bottom of the lake and he's going to break the surface of the water and keep on going, all the way up into the sky and through into outer space. Only two ways a body can disappear and one of them is magic.

They got to find him, not because of any reward or for anybody's dad or mom, they got to find him because he's all alonely out here. He's got no name and nobody's missing him and that's just, that's just a Hell of a Thing.

'Get up.' He's shaking Emilia. 'We found him.' She's still snoring so he shakes her harder. But when he turns back, the man isn't breaking the surface, isn't heading for outer space. He's sinking again, back down to the bottom, shrinking into Elwy's eye, hair waving as he goes. Goodbye.

Emilia wakes to the sound of Elwy whistling, not a ghost at all. She never would've thought, her best friend in the world, a real whistler. And she doesn't hush him, she just lets him go on and on. Forever if he wants.

12

Fuck this place.

Fuck that guy and his boots.

Fuck me.

Fuck my nose, fuck this blood. Fuck this hurts.

Fuck Francie for leaving me. Fuck Heck wherever he fuckin is. Fuck Martha and her stupid waitress job and all her stupid waitress friends. Fuck her for waiting on Van and fuck him too and all the years without him.

Fuck this acid.

Fuck photography. Fuck art. Fuck making a difference. Fuck trying to change people, trying to affect things. Fuck beauty.

A universe of fucks, a lifetime of fucks, fucks stretching off to infinity. Fuck is the limit of what Slim Slider can think, say or feel as he pulls himself up off the mattress and tries to find something to wipe all this blood off his face. A triangle of broken mirror hanging on the wall tells him he looks like shit. Worse shit than usual. He touches his nose. It's practically the worst pain he's ever felt but he's pretty sure it's not broken.

He uses the edge of the blanket to clean his face and then digs around until he finds a pair of his old red Chucks lying in the corner. Lacing them up on the mattress, looking around this place – his place. The paint already starting to flake, and him and Francie just painted it in the summer. Yellow, she said, like margarine on toast.

Him and Francie, Slim and Francie – there, a photo of the two of them hung up with a tack, taken at the folk festival down at the lake. His arm around Francie, her smiling so big her face might crack. A good day in the middle of a bunch of good ones.

Fuck the good days.

He pulls the tack out and brings the picture closer, closer, so close he gets a soft whiff of vinegar from the photographic paper. So close he's staring into the faces of Slim and Francie a year younger and trying to find the story of how those people back then become us now. Slim and Francie carving their names on all the rocks and benches all over town with hearts around them. Slim and Francie leaving town in the red Dart, heading for fame in the big city. Slim and Francie still stuck here, the snow settling down around them, suffocating them in another hard winter in this cold town.

He puts the photo back up, jabs the tack straight through his heart. Outside the slag is cooling off and the shack is going dark, the orange light fading across the wall. Slim and Francie fading away. Francie out there god knows where with his jacket, Slim lying back on this mattress as the dark comes down. Fuck Francie. Fuck Slim.

A loud *crack*. The window above him shatters, glass showering him as he instinctively covers his eyes. He thinks, Rock, somebody threw a rock, that asshole with the boots came back – but then another *crack* and a hole appears in the wall at the foot of the mattress. Through it, he can see the black hills ringing the shacks, the snow coating the ridge.

And up there, a small flash from the snow, then another *crack*. A hot whisper by his left ear and the photo of Slim and Francie is torn in two.

He rolls off the mattress, glass crunching beneath him, cutting parts of him he'll feel later. He grabs the Polaroid bag off the chair and vaults through the broken window.

He hits the ground and leans his back against the tin siding of the shack, waiting for more *crack*s but none come. Holding the camera against his chest like it's a pistol and him Lee Marvin. A dim orange glow from the slag hangs for a minute and then fizzles. He waits for the cover of darkness before he creeps to the corner of the shack.

He peeks around the edge. Scanning the ridge, looking for any sign. Nothing. He ducks back and fumbles through the camera bag, coming out with an old zoom. He holds the lens up to the Polaroid iris with shaking hands.

He leans out again, bringing the camera up this time, pressing the viewfinder to his eye. He goes left to right, searching for any movement, any shape in all that slag. He's shaking all over the place and he balls his right hand tight to kill the tremor. But his finger catches the shutter and off goes the flash.

Up on the ridge he gets the strobe of an answer and the *crack* follows after. Something hits the ground about two feet in front of him, kicking a handful of dirt up in his face. He spins back around the edge of the building. Behind him all that slag and somebody trying to kill him, straight ahead the lights of Gatchell just over the horizon. Ready or not here I come. He puts his head down and runs, thinking about Lee Marvin dodging bullets in any war movie he'd seen back when they still had money to rent a VCR.

He crosses the highway, slides on his ass into the ditch and then breaks for the Delki Dozzi complex, following the chain-link and staying away from the open field, the baseball diamond, skirting the tennis courts and making for the shadows around the clubhouse.

He pushes through into the sick yellow dim of a washroom. Across stained tile and into a stall, closing the door and turning the latch. He sits on the toilet seat and pulls his feet up after him. He tries to focus on the smell of old piss, the graffiti all over the stall, the clunking sound of the water pipes – anything to stop waiting to hear the door open.

He pulls a marker out of his pocket, pops the cap and starts doodling on the wall. Writing *Slim plus* – and he's going to put *Francie*, out of habit, purely out of habit. But fuck Francie. Slim plus nothing.

They could be in Toronto right now. Out of here. On the way to anything else. If they'd accepted him at the art school. If Francie hadn't gone apeshit. If the acid hadn't been bad. If Heck hadn't blabbed. If that asshole hadn't found him and taken the boots. If if if – if everyone and everything else hadn't fucked up.

There's the groan of the washroom door and his lungs choke up. Footsteps across the tile, one, two, three, so loud in this quiet, four, five, and stopping right outside the stall. Slim closes his eyes, waiting for the *crack*. The *crack* and then the end, wondering if it'll hurt and if Francie will cry when she finds out.

'Slim?'

Not a *crack*, but a whisper. He opens his eyes. Two shoes standing outside the stall. Two too-familiar white high-tops. 'Heck?'

'Fuckin jeepers, Slim, I thought it was you but I wasn't sure.' The stall door rattling. 'Hey, open up.'

'Keep your fuckin voice down, Heck.'

'Yeah, yeah, sure thing.' The door rattling again, Heck whining, 'C'mon, man, lemme in.'

'I told you to leave me alone.'

'Aw, c'mon, man – I was worried. I was down by your place, watchin the car in case – then I got nervous so I headed up to the hideout.'

'What for?'

'Told you – I was worried.'

'Why?'

'Cause of Francie and all that and the way you tore off.'

'That's why you're worried.'

'Yeah, man.' The door rattling like a sack of bones. 'And that bad acid.' Heck's greasy mullet pokes through under the door, squirming in with his big shiny ski vest like a slug. 'What happened to your face?'

'Someone's trying to kill me.'

'You got into another fight?'

'No – yeah, but now someone's trying to kill me – with a gun.'

'Aw, man.' Heck bursts immediately, big tears coming down his cheeks, only the ten millionth time he's seen his friend cry. 'I'm,' sob, 'fuckin,' sob, 'sorry,' big sob, 'Slim.'

'What're you sorry for?'

'I went back to Top Hat for some Rygar and that's where he found me – I don't know how he knew me and I didn't want to say nothin – '

'Who?'

' – but all he did was look at me and I swear – I fuckin swear, Slim, his eyes were red – no fuckin lie – just like they said, and one look and I knew he was gonna kill me right there – my guts all over Rygar and ten quarters in – '

'Fuck – who, Heck? Who?'

' – so I fuckin spilled it, Slim – I told him about the hideout and he just walked out – '

'Who?'

'Milly.'

Slim feels his heart stop – it just literally fuckin quits on him – and he leans back, hitting the handle, and the toilet goes off, water thundering and him and Heck both scream. Thank fuck at least it gets his heart started up again.

'Jyrki fuckin Myllarinen.' And he whispers it, like a ghost story, like the name of the bogeyman, like any louder and he might pop right out of the drain and kill them both.

Heck sits on the piss-coated floor, the silence drawing long and tight, ready to snap until he can't take it anymore. 'You think it's true what they say he did to his parents?'

'I dunno.'

'Into little bits? With a hacksaw?'

'I don't fuckin know, Heck.'

'I thought it was total bullshit, but then I saw him. He's big, Slim, like seven feet – '

'He's not seven feet.'

'He's big, man. And I think he's got red eyes, just like they said.'

'Okay.' Saying it like cut-the-bullshit and stands up like he's got a plan.

Heck looks up at him with big eyes. 'What's *okay*? Nothing's okay, man.'

'We're gonna go for the car.'

'You can't go out there.'

'Well, we can't sit on the toilet all fuckin night.' Heck starts the waterworks again. 'Look – we'll be quick, stick to backyards.'

'Where're we gonna go – the cops?'

'No way.' He pulls Heck to his feet, all sloppy and dripping.

'Where?'

'I'll figure it out.'

'Aw, man – I don't wanna fuckin die.' Heck sinks to the floor again.

'Cool it.' He twists the latch and swings the door open, going to the cracked mirror to look at himself. 'He's after me – not you.'

'Oh yeah.' Heck pulls himself up, relieved – almost happy.

Slim runs some water and rinses the rest of the blood off, wipes his arms where the glass bit in and pulls that lock of hair down to cover the black eye that's forming.

'Slim?' Heck still lingering in the stall, like he's at home base in there. 'Why're we in the girls' washroom?'

They jump the sagging fence into the backyard of Slim's apartment building – everything quiet. They slip up the laneway and peer out at the street, snow still piling up and no footprints anyplace. Houses up and down the street sleeping in the blue glow of the TV. The red Dart sitting there, waiting for them.

'I wish your mom was home.' Heck looking at the dark windows on the first floor.

'Why?'

'I dunno. She's your mom. Maybe she could do something.'

'Well, she's at work – so shut up.'

Slim crouches, giving Heck the signal to hold back, and scampers for the car. Pulling the door open, sliding inside. Then waving Heck in beside him.

The car purrs and they roll out onto Logan and down the street. He keeps an eye on the rear-view, but no one's back there. He catches his puffy eyes and reaches into the glovebox and grabs his Wayfarers. When they get to the edge of Lorne, the traffic's running thick in both directions and he breathes out. He swings a left and they sink into the crowd. Olly olly oxen free.

The snow smacking wet across the windshield, the wipers clearing everything but that little white shark fin in the centre. The car coasting like a boat across the slush – winter tires still wrapped up in plastic in the basement – and Slim's thoughts coasting with it.

The Polaroid on his lap like a baby. Trying to remember the last time he took a photo. The last real one. Not the stupid smiling pictures he took for Francie's cousin's wedding. Not the yearbook poses he let Mr. K talk him into taking. Something real. Something that was here and gone, caught in that split second.

Never should've applied for that stupid art school in the first place. Never should've let her talk him into it. Sure, she said all the right things, said she loved his stuff, said he could be famous or whatever, anything he wanted – but he doesn't even know what the fuck he wants. Who does?

Francie sleeping in the shack at the end of summer. Her bare shoulder, a curl of brown hair around her ear. Tip of one thumb curved toward her lips, open just a crack. The instant before her eyelid would rise, before she was there awake and all that truth would just fold up.

That was the last real one he took.

He comes back to feel a clunking underneath him – something giving on the right side of the car. He slows down and takes the next left, Heck immediately twitching in his seat. 'Why're you turnin here?'

'Feels like a flat.'

'Aw, man, you gotta be shitting me.'

He pulls them down a short drive, out of sight from the street, and turns off the ignition. They hop out. Heck shivering while Slim checks. 'Aren't you cold?'

Slim looks down at his T-shirt. 'Nope.'

'You're gonna get sick.'

'Yeah, I'm real worried about a sore throat right now. How's your side?'

'Fine.' Heck looks down for the first time. 'Fuuuck.'

'What is it?' Slim comes around to the other side of the car, following Heck's stare down to the front tire, brick flat, a square of white and something black sticking out of it. He grabs and pulls. The shine of metal – a switchblade – the square of folded paper coming with it.

'What's it say?'

He unfolds the paper. Four words, each letter formed very carefully in black ink so there'll be no mistake. *My brother before midnight.*

He gives it to Heck, who reads it and then keeps reading it like some great mystery will come popping out. He fingers the knife, pulling the hasp and the blade jumps back into the handle. Heck looking up at the sound. 'What're we gonna do?'

He slips the switchblade into his pocket and throws Heck the keys. 'Spare's in the trunk.'

'What? I'm not gettin it.' Heck looks to the back of the car. 'There was a dead guy back there.'

'Get the fuckin spare, Heck.'

'And then what? Then we go drive around some more? We can't go back to your place – he knows where you live. He knows your car. You don't wanna go to the cops. So what're we gonna do – wait for him to find us?'

'We're gonna flip the tire.' He sits down on the hood, looking out at the line of tall naked poplars waving in the wind. The creek below. Back here behind Wembley Public, and he didn't even know that's where he was driving the whole time. 'And then we're gonna go find that body.'

They slide down the bank by the bridge and follow the trail all the way to the black mouth of the culvert. Heck kicking at the snow and sulking the whole way. 'This is a bad idea, Slim,' like a broken record.

It's a half-moon of old brick, sagging like busted teeth, holding up the road above them, traffic running over, the water running slow and dark underneath. He gets right up to the edge and spots a small ledge not more than two feet wide running off into the black. Heck at his shoulder, peering past. A warm exhalation of air runs over them.

'How far does it go?'

'I dunno.' Slim playing with the flashlight, pushing the button, not getting anything. 'The creek runs under half the city. They buried it up years ago.'

'Isn't this where Normando used to bring kids and eat them?'

'Don't be a wastoid – those're just stories.'

'Well, there better not be any bats or cannibal hobos in there. I don't got my tetanus shot.'

Slim smacks the flashlight against the edge of the culvert, warm light flickering on, and pulls off the sunglasses. 'C'mon.'

They shuffle forward, following the beam of the flashlight, playing across the ledge, the concrete walls, the dripping ceiling, the water. Slim's nostrils fill with damp and mould. He takes one look over his shoulder to see the circle of street light receding behind them, shrinking to a penny.

There's a rumbling overhead and Heck jumps forward, almost knocking him in the water. 'Chill – it's just the cars.'

'Yeah, sorry, man.'

Slim keeps the light moving across the creek, looking for any sign – a hand, the pale glow of flesh. Reflections off the water making shivering ghosts on the concrete.

The tunnel bends to the left and he steals one last look back – a pinhole of dying light. Two more steps and it's gone.

'Slim?'

'Mm.'

'What're we gonna do if we find it?'

'Bring it back.'

'Yeah, cool. Why?'

'Give it to Milly.'

'And then he'll stop shooting you.'

'That's the plan.'

'Thought you didn't know if it's his brother anyway.'

'Well ... he seems pretty sure.'

The air is getting tighter here, older, and he can feel the ceiling dropping down on them, so close now it forces them to stoop. There's another gust of warm air across his face, like this place is alive, like it's been waiting for them.

'Y'know what I heard? I heard after he killed his parents he used their bones to make furniture – like chairs and shit.'

'Stop spitting on my neck.' He remembers Mr. Oliver's history class. Some lecture about the catacombs in Paris. A grainy slide, hundreds of skulls arranged in the pattern of a heart. The light flickers and he slaps it until it comes back strong.

A faint sound is growing, like the snow on a dead TV channel, and the ceiling continues to drop. Slim gets down on all fours, swinging the camera to his back. 'We're gonna have to crawl.'

Heck mumbles something that sounds like *Bad idea*, but grunts along behind him all the same. The light bobs ahead as he crawls – more ledge, more water, stretching on. It makes him dizzy and he concentrates on his watch instead. Bringing him back like it always has, like that one bubble of focus in a photo, everything blurring around it. All the shit he's been through, least he's always had this. Gold plated. Speedmaster – the one the astronauts wore, Van used to say when he let Slim hold it – a moonwatch. The watch reminding him this is who and where you are – you are Slim Slider, you are in some seriously deep shit, but you've got a chance. Find that body.

Heck shrieks and jolts him from behind – making him lose his grip on the flashlight and there it goes, splashing into the water. He reaches for it – too late – the water glowing sick and green as it sinks, sinks, hits the bottom and dies. Darkness.

Heck whimpers behind him. Slim kicks at him. 'Smooth move, Ex-Lax.'

'Something touched my leg, man!'

'Probably just a fuckin rat.'

'Don't joke, I hate rats – you know I hate fuckin rats, man!'

'Shut up.'

'What're we gonna do now?'

He kicks out again. 'Shut the fuck up.'

The dead TV sound has continued to grow – now a *whoosh*ing – and he can feel a warm spray, like spit, on his face. He looks down at his watch – the hands glowing faint in the dark. He shuffles forward again, deeper into the thick dark.

'Hey – where're you goin?'

'A bit farther.'

Another whimper. 'But we can't see nothin.'

'Wanna go back for your Teddy Ruxpin?'

They squirm on, Slim humming under his breath, losing all sense of distance, time and direction. The culvert seems like years ago already, and they might be a hundred kilometres down to the centre of the earth or just a few dozen feet from the entrance. He realizes he's humming that Rick Wakeman album that always used to give him nightmares. The electronic notes and images of giant glowing mushrooms ringing in the dark.

The stone is coated in slime here, like the diving rocks down at the lake. There's something old about this place, older than the concrete around them. Men on their bellies digging for gold and finding nickel instead. He's heard that the entire downtown has enough ore in it to keep the place going forever, but they'd have to blow it all up to get at it.

The sound is now a thundering and it's close, so close they're almost inside it. Maybe the water drops off here. A pool where things gather – it might be right here. He pushes forward another foot and hits something, hard and stuck. He yells back at Heck, 'Hold on!'

He runs his hands over the grit of rust and cold metal – iron bars. A grate of some kind blocking their way forward. Stopping them this close. He slams a fist into the bars, but it doesn't give.

The face of his watch glows. Find the body. Find the girl.

Fuck focus.

He squeezes his arm through the bars. Reaching up, trying to find some latch or lock. Nothing. He stretches out, feeling the stone ahead, pressing up against the bars – reaching as far as he can.

Something grabs his hand.

Something out of the thunder, out of the slime, out of the darkness.

He pulls back, his hand slipping loose, scraping through the bars and falling back against Heck. Lifting his camera as he falls, the flash going off. In that split second, that dying moment, he's not sure but he thinks he sees something – pale naked flesh beyond the bars, two globes of light in the flash. Like the eyeshine of an animal in a photograph. Here and gone. Hello, darkness.

He lies back into the warm and soft of Heck. Sinking into the darkness and maybe it's shock but his mind again kicks up Mr. Oliver's lecture – tunnels in the catacombs that were walled up and people left inside. Buried alive.

Just like this. Just enough space to get the whiff of fresh air. Then slam a grate down. Grates on every side of you, burying you into a life before you've had a chance to choose. Give them the time and they'd brick the whole thing up, him and Heck with it.

He realizes he's being pulled back and he fights the entire length of black until they're out in the air again. The cold like a slap across his face. Heck tosses him on the ground and leans over gasping. 'Are you mental?'

Looking up at the street above, the glow of lampposts like a Lite-Brite board. 'Didn't you see it?'

'See what? I couldn't see anything past your ass, man.'

'It was right there, on the other side of the grate.'

'What was?'

'The body!'

'What? But how would it get through the grate?'

'I dunno. Maybe there's a hole underwater.'

'I don't think so, man.'

'Then maybe there's another way through.'

Heck's face scrunches up. 'And how would it get there?'

'Something grabbed me, Heck. I felt it.'

The street light flickers off and then on. They both start to shiver.

'Like no way, m-m-man.' Heck stammers in the cold. 'That's not possible.'

Slim looks down and sees the Polaroid still hanging from the lips of the camera. 'I snapped a picture of it.'

'Lemme see.' Heck grabs the photo, brings it right to his nose and then relaxes. 'You dick. I thought you were for real – that's not funny, man.' He chucks the photo at Slim and heads back up the bank to the car.

Slim holding the photo, the bars of the grate lit up by a flash, nothing beyond it but the black secret water no one would see because they brick up anything real and alive.

Back in the Dart, both of them stinking like ditch water. The note on the dash. *My brother before midnight*. And Slim's moonwatch says it's already past eight.

Heck stops chewing his fingernails long enough to spit a few out on the upholstery. 'No cops.'

'Nope.'

'No body.'

'Nope.'

'No plan.'

'Nope.'

'Totally not cool, man.' Back to chewing his nails.

'I just need some time.'

'To what – become bulletproof?'

'To think.'

'Okay, well, we can't go to your place and I'm not bringing you over to my house so my parents can get shot at. Oh shit!' He pats his pockets and pulls out two small squares of paper. 'I totally forgot – my mom got me tickets to see this Victor guy.'

'Who?'

'He's a peenist.'

'A penis?'

'No, shit for brains, a pee-nist – y'know, like Mozart. Anyway, he's at the Grand – show's already started, but we could catch the second half.'

'I'm gettin shot at and you wanna go to the theatre?'

'C'mon – there'll be lots of people around, it'll be safe. And it'll give you time to think … or whatever.' He shoves the tickets at him like he's going to tear them then and there. 'You got any better ideas?'

The lobby's empty, their footsteps echoing across the granite, scaring a mouse back into a hole gnawed through the thick wood panelling. Slim listens to the door and hears music, so they sneak into the dark theatre. The smell of old popcorn and mothballs.

A spotlight is on a little man in a tuxedo sitting at a giant piano. He's banging away, none of the notes in tune with each other. 'This guy sucks,' Slim whispers, but then everybody laughs and he wonders what he's not getting.

Some pimply usher he recognizes from the high school makes a big deal out of being all official and taking their tickets, making them wait while he gets his little penlight working. He leads them over ancient carpet down to their seats, right near the front. Heck muttering a thousand *scuse mes* as he wriggles in.

The man onstage stops playing to glare down at them and cracks something about starting over again and everyone yuks it up. Slim feels himself going red like he always does when he's the centre of attention. He leans over to Heck. 'This was a bad idea.'

The piano man goes back to attacking the keys. It's real classical stuff, like what you hear at Christmas or in doctors' offices, but everyone seems to be enjoying it. Then he makes a big dramatic gesture and falls off the bench.

Everybody laughs – just like that – because this guy fell on his ass, and sure he looks okay as he gets back up, but it's cruel. People are the same all over.

And just like that, he's off the bench again, *kerplunk*, and looking all surprised. This time it's even more hilarious to everyone – the woman beside him laughing so hard she starts coughing, big wet phlegm on her fat lips. People're the same. Laughing at this little old geezer with his thin moustache. Laughing more the more he falls, the more he hurts. Laughing when you're down, laughing when you fuck up cause they'd never fuck up. Laughing when you piss your pants in Grade 1. When your dad leaves, cause they all knew he was no good to begin with. When you wear the same clothes all week cause your mom can't afford new ones. When you say you want to be a photographer, cause you're supposed to be a mucker, or if you're any good laughing cause what the fuck good is a photograph. When your girl leaves you, when your best friend's sick of you, when you got nowhere left to turn – when you're finally face down, full of bullet holes and dying, there they'll be standing over you, laughing. Cause you never were any good. People are cruel all over. Well, fuck em.

The piano man's on the floor a third time and they're howling, rolling in the aisles, even Heck now, and it makes you so sick you want to jump up in the middle of the whole theatre, stand tall like Lee Marvin against the mob and say, Stop it! Stop laughin at him, you fuckin sickos!

But you don't cause they only do that in the movies and the thought of it all stopping and everyone looking, the spectacle of it, makes you want to cover your face cause it's so fuckin embarrassing to be alive.

The piano man gets up, flips up the lid of the bench and pulls out two straps, metal clattering. A seat belt. He sits down and straps himself in.

And so even this little frail old geezer is part of the joke. Fuck it all.

His head throbs and he looks down at his watch. Arms stretching out, but even that's not inviting because all it's saying is three hours – less than three hours left.

'Do you like good music?'

He looks up – it's the piano man. Seat belt off, he's at the front of the stage, looking down at Slim, holding some pages against his chest. Not accusing, not making fun, and although there's a twinkle in his eye, it's kind. It sets Slim at ease, he doesn't turn red.

'Do you like good music?' the little man asks again.

'Uh, yeah – sure.' He says it real quiet, but the piano man smiles, big and friendly, and leans down, holding out the papers. Offering. Slim reaches forward and takes them, and for a moment the piano man holds on, seems about to say something else. Maybe make a joke. But instead he just lets go, turns back to the piano and straps himself in again.

Slim looks down at the papers – sheet music. Hungarian something by Franz somebody he's never heard of before. But down at the bottom of the page is a note in messy handwriting. *The shortest distance between two people*. And that's it.

Is what? It's missing something. Did this little man, back playing more music that makes the audience go *haw haw*, did he write it for him? What is the shortest distance between two people?

Van as far away from him as a person can get. Martha a few blocks away down at the diner, but in some ways as far away from him as Van. Heck two inches to his right and his best friend, sure, but does he really know him? Then Francie.

All the naked of Francie stretched out next to him in the shack in the summer, bodies stuck by sweat, sunk down deep into each other. This the shortest distance.

Heck elbows him. 'This guy's fuckin hilarious!'

And Slim tries to laugh, tries to laugh with everybody laughing around him, tries to be in on this. But he's never felt so far away from everything. Everybody.

Francie out there god knows where and that distance growing by the minute.

All the way back down Beech, Heck's going on about how great the show was, but something is nagging at Slim. Something more than the time ticking down on his left wrist. Maybe it's the dead-quiet night – no breeze at all. Even Heck seems to feel it, shutting up as they pass the church, the big dark pines silent and still, the rose window dark. It's only when they're both back in the Dart that he realizes what it is. The snow's finally stopped.

The street is empty. Their footprints leading back the only sign that anyone has been down here. Like the entire world had been put on pause, everything waiting on something to drop.

He turns the key, the engine rumbling awake. He flicks the headlights on – and back at the top of the hill, a pair of lights answers.

Just someone else from the concert, and he waits for the car to turn around or approach, but it doesn't move. It just sits there. The perfectly round headlights staring down, and there's something unnerving about it, the way a hunk of metal can feel alive like that.

'Let's get out of here, Slim.'

He puts the car in gear and starts to crawl up the hill. Just pass it on by – but then those headlights start their own crawl down. Swinging over to their lane.

'Slim.' Not panic in Heck's voice but riding the edge.

Slim reverses the car back down to the bottom, spinning her around, so she's facing up Durham now. Out Heck's window he can see the other car advancing on them, slow but deliberate. Yellow – a Beetle. He leans over, trying to get a better look. 'Who is that?'

'Who gives a fuck – let's go.'

He puts the car back in gear and gives her gas. The wheels spin. He gives it more, but he can see the slush being kicked up in the rear-view.

'Slim!'

The Beetle's high beams pop on and the car is flooded with light. Slim grabs a handful of Heck's vest and twists him toward the back seat. 'Get your fat ass back there!'

Heck throws himself over the console and lands in a heap in the back. Slim rides the brake and opens her up, feeling the wheels finally bite down on something, the ass of the Dart fishtailing up Durham. He winces, thinking about the spare.

'Go, go!' Heck on his knees peering out the back window.

In the mirror he catches the Beetle making the corner and following in their wake, gaining speed. He gives Elm a quick scan as he's pulling up and then blasts on through.

'Slim – it's one-way!'

'Let's see the fucker follow us.'

But the fucker does follow them, some car honking and swerving through the slush to avoid the Beetle as it also cuts across Elm. At the end of the long straight stretch ahead, Slim sees another car pull onto Durham facing him, but he blows the next intersection anyway and keeps on.

Some drunk stumbles off the sidewalk into the road, Heck yelling, 'Watch out!' and Slim has to jerk the wheel to the left to avoid clipping him. The Dart hops the curb, then comes back down with a crash, Heck flopping around in the back seat.

The oncoming car now one block on and closing – that driver's head so far up his ass he hasn't seen them yet. Slim steals a look at the mirror – the Beetle right there behind him, sandwiching them in.

'Look out!'

Heck's shout brings him back – another intersection, a truck turning onto Durham. Slim screeches around it, the driver's mouth hanging open as they pass, and then he yanks back to the right to avoid the next car. The shriek of metal and he watches his side mirror tear off.

Just ahead the road ends with a hard left onto Elgin. He guns it – Heck's shout pitching up – and pulls on the handbrake, steering into the turn, the ass of the Dart drifting, pulling the nose back the other way, and then opening the throttle as they straighten out onto the thoroughfare.

Heck's crying or laughing back there now.

The car jolts – something hitting them from behind, and Slim checks the rear-view – the big globes of the Beetle trying to climb in through the back window.

He flashes the brakes, hoping it will throw this guy off, but instead the Beetle veers into the oncoming lane and, with a snarl, pulls up beside them, going neck and neck down past the Friendly, May's, the Nickel Bin – giving the drunks something to look at.

The Beetle inches over, sparks flying as they touch. He pulls as far to the curb as he can, but in comes the yellow car again. He looks over, making out the dark shape of a man. A hand coming up, a finger pointed at him. *You.*

Slim swerves left and slams into the Beetle, sending it up over the curb and rolling across the grass outside the arena, cracking into one of the concrete planters. He pulls back into his lane and jams the pedal to the floor, his body thrown back as the Dart rages forward. He blows the red on Paris and sails into traffic.

And it's in slow motion and he's as cool as Lee Marvin in *Point Blank*, the lights from all angles the horns the screeching, and then he opens his eyes and they're across, climbing the hill on Van Horne.

He takes a hard right off the main drag up a dark gravel lane. Pulls them into a tiny lot behind some trees and shuts it all down.

Waits. But no one's coming.

'Aw, jinkies.' Heck coughs in the back seat. 'I puked all over the place.'

They get out and follow the winding path up into the Grotto, passing the big granite statues of people in togas in various states of agony. Agony maybe at the ground littered with broken beer bottles and grocery bags.

They reach the top and sit underneath the glowing neon cross.

The lights of downtown twisted out before them. Slim picks up a handful of gravel and starts chucking stones at a little porcelain sculpture of the Virgin Mary.

Heck's holding his belly like he's been gut-shot. 'I'm so hungry I'd eat Normando's popcorn, boogers and all. You got anything to eat?'

Slim digs around in his pockets and comes out with a green sucker, tosses it over. 'Try not to barf it back up.'

Heck pulls off the wrapper and pops the sucker in his mouth, crunching away at it. 'So ... you think that was Milly?'

Slim gives him a look to let him know how stupid he is.

'Well, I dunno! How much time we got left?'

Slim checks the moonwatch. 'Just over an hour.'

'Fuuuck.' He watches Slim hit Mary, a piece of her cheek cracking off. 'Don't do that, man.'

'Fuck off, Heck – you're not Catholic.'

'It's bad luck.' Heck tosses the dead sucker stick away.

'So's littering.'

Heck leans back against the cross, the red neon glow washing across his face. 'So what're you gonna do?'

'Nothin.' Slim standing and flinging the whole handful down at the city. 'All my life, Heck – one big nothin.'

'C'mon, man – it'll work out ... somehow.'

'Really? Then tell me what to do.'

'Maybe you could take him on – y'know.' Heck stretches one arm up. 'I have the power!' He snorts it off.

'I'm serious.' Slim sitting down beside his friend, looking him in the face and really asking. 'What do I do?'

Heck swallows his laugh and comes back at him with this look. 'I dunno.'

'I'm so fucked, Heck.'

And the look opens up even more and Slim gets it. Disappointment. He always has the answers, but not this time.

Heck shrugs. 'Maybe you could talk to this guy – explain it to him.'

'Jyrki fuckin Myllarinen? He tries to shoot me, run me off the road – I don't think he's that into talking.'

'Well, get out of town then.'

'No, I'm done with that. He wants to find me, he'll find me.'

'So what do you want – you wanna die, man?'

Bullet through his head, his car flying off the Paris Street bridge, beaten and kicked until everything's broken and bleeding – all the ends of Slim, none of them good. None fit. Like the way Slim and Francie fit. They'd have had dinner at that Mexican place, and now they'd be walking Yonge Street, floating on all the light and noise. Out of here. On the way to something. If he hadn't stolen those boots. If he hadn't sold his gear. If he hadn't taken that body. If he hadn't fucked things up with Francie. If he'd only tried harder. If if if – if only. They'd be on their way, the two of them. Good days for all the days left. It's his fault. All his fault.

'Let's go.'

'But what about – ?'

'Fuck Milly and the fuckin body and all the rest of it. Fuck it all.'

He pulls the Wayfarers out of his pocket and slaps them on, heading back down the hill, cutting it all loose. But there Heck is, right at his shoulder. 'Where're we goin?'

'I'm gonna find Francie.'

And down they go, that cross burning in neon behind them for someone else to bear.

The streets and faces and places swim in front of Slim. They're at Top Hat with the skids, at the Cotton Club with the mods, at the Marymount stairs with the potheads, at the pizza place outside the mall with the scenesters, the smeared bus shelters on Lisgar with the rest. He sees her down an alley, catches her perfume on the breeze, hears her laugh, but every time he looks she's gone. They're everywhere and Francie's nowhere.

Finally, they find some punk kids from school having a snowball fight in the cement square outside the government buildings, one of them saying, 'Yeah, I seen her at the Nash earlier.'

'When?'

'Coupla hours ago. Said she was headed to the Bin to see some shitty blues band.'

'The Bin – thanks.'

And they're off, cutting through Memorial, and Slim's just about to make the break across Brady when Heck grabs him and pulls him back into the shadows of the trees at the edge of the park.

'What?'

Heck pointing across the way – a yellow Beetle in the parking lot behind the arena. They just watch, not saying anything for a few minutes. Heck finally coughs like he's been holding his breath the whole time. 'You think he's in there?'

'I dunno – maybe.'

'What time is it?'

Slim looks down at his watch. A minute to midnight. A minute to midnight the last time he checked too. 'I dunno. Must be almost two in the morning.' The piece of shit broken. A moonwatch – bullshit – even the gold plating had long since scratched away showing the metal underneath. Reminding him this is who and where you are – cheap, Slim, a big cheap fake. Slim Slider not even your real name. 'Look, I'm gonna go cut back through the alley and work my way back over to Elgin.'

'Okay, cool, let's go.'

'Nope. We split here.'

Heck blinking, hurt. 'Why?'

'Cause I said so.' Cause they can both feel the shit is about to get deeper. 'Cause you're slowing me down.' Cause I don't want you to get hurt – he doesn't say it, makes it easy for both of them, and Heck doesn't say so either, but for once he gets it, and he looks relieved.

Heck walks slowly to a park bench and sits down. 'I'll just … sit here for a bit – you can shout if you need me.'

Slim flashes a smile, one he almost feels. 'Captain Barfbag to the rescue.'

And there they are, awkward like that for a minute, and then without thinking Slim takes off the watch and tosses it to Heck, who catches it like it's the Holy fuckin Grail.

'Wowsers, man. This is your watch – your dad gave it to you.'

He looks down at his wrist, the pale skin there, the line where the strap bit in – only taking it off to shower all these years. Slim Novak or Slim Slider – the same Slim. 'Van didn't give it to me,' he laughs, and it's the first real thing that's happened all day. 'He left it behind. Like he did with everything.' Even left his name behind like a husk of snakeskin.

And before anything can take the cruel beautiful truth of that away, he spins hard and walks off, closing the distance.

13

Normando is staring at the ceiling above the bed by the time the moon sneaks in through the shutters. Pat's breath whistles through her nose and Norm rolls to look at her. Hair snaking in grey drifts across her pillow, creased forehead let loose with sleep – some kind of peace.

His eyes trace the line of her neck, down to her shoulder and beyond, the nightstand and the black-bordered picture frame, turned facedown. He knows the photograph – the white flash of teeth in the smile of the young boy there, the miner's helmet sinking low over his ears.

When he worked late, some nights he would sneak into the boy's room and ease onto the end of the mattress, knowing the boy was only pretending, that he'd heard the truck pull in, the latch on the front door. Normando would whisper a story about the damned mine – how he found a cockroach in his lunch pail or the time Ristimaki lost one of his boots down a pit and had to jump around on one leg like an arsehole. Normando jumping around the room to demonstrate, light on his toes and shushing the boy's laughter so's not to wake Pat.

The boy liked to hear the one about the time he saved the two Italians from a cave-in. Went back down because he counted two short and moved the rocks all by himself. Nobody believed he could've done it. The boy loved that Normando would show him how big the rocks were with his hands and each time the rocks would get a little bigger. The boy would tease him about this because he remembered. Because he listened.

Normando slides his skinny old bow legs out from under the sheets, pads off down the hall, Pat whistling through her nose like a kettle behind him.

14

It's not even 2 a.m. when the amp blows and it's not because they're playing too loud but because their equipment's so old. Moony Bedard turns to the rest of the guys to see if they want to keep going acoustic, but the drummer Lepine says, 'My hemorrhoids hurt and I wanna go home.' Half done murdering a Franglais cover of 'The Thrill Is Gone' and the evening's over.

The house music comes on to cover for them, but the twenty or so people who turned up for the gig barely register the changeover. Moony packs up the bass and by the time they've got the van loaded Stef is already asleep in the passenger side. They all stand on the pavement looking at each other, Lepine dancing from one foot to the other trying to stay warm, Felix with his hands in his pockets and Stef, drooling, face pressed against the glass in the background. Moony says, 'Well,' and the other guys say, 'Well,' and they all nod a bit more and then Moony says, 'Well,' again, but with more finality.

After the van takes off, Moony heads back inside, making straight for the bar and giving Foisey the nod. The bartender slides a rum and coke across, saying, 'This's the last of your rider. Sorry, Moony.'

He turns and leans against the bar, pulling off his ball cap and running a hand over the smooth dome of his skull. *Le thrill est parti.* Only a handful of people left but the place is still smoky as hell. In the old days someone would've already been up to buy him a drink. He thinks about going to talk to the cute brunette in the denim jacket who seemed to be paying attention most of the night. Then a cheer comes up from the table of mouthbreathers who kept requesting Slayer covers and he just feels sick instead.

The men's room has indoor plumbing but you wouldn't know it from the smell. He goes to the last urinal and stands with his hands on his hips, dangling, waiting for the release. A poster right at eye level, *BayBay Roi,* a younger version of himself with more hair and a darker moustache looking back at him. All of them, Stef, Lepine and Felix, looking so goddamn happy. *Ten Year Reunion.*

Some reunion. Stef's voice was shit, couldn't hit the high notes, Felix kept losing his place and Lepine ... well, he was as bad as ever. They all had to be dragged out for this pretty much kicking and screaming and Moony doesn't know why he bothered. They used to get one, maybe two, hundred on a good night. Have all their fans died? Maybe just gone senile.

A stall door bangs open and some other old bastard, wiping his hands on his pants, takes one look at Moony. 'Didn't you fuckers have a ten-year reunion ten years ago?'

'You gonna wash your hands, Lo?'

Lorenzo flicks his fingers at him, like he's flinging shit, and stands with his big grin while Moony tries to piss. 'Y'know, we were gonna have a reunion too – but I called around and found out Marco died. Heart attack. Hadn't talked to him in years.'

'You could never play worth shit anyway.' Moony grunts, a few drops. 'Emilia was talkin in class again today.'

'Oh yeah?' Lorenzo sits on the counter next to the sink, getting comfortable. 'You goin to Fitzroy's later?'

'That damn rasta still runnin the speakeasy?' Grunt, drip drip.

'People still have after-parties, don't they?'

'Guess I gotta celebrate the end of BayBay Roi somewhere, eh?' Grunt, a trickle.

The door swings open and one of the mouthbreathers comes in, his pants already unbuckled, ready to scoop himself into any available drain. With the entire row free, he staggers all the way down right next to Moony, immediately letting loose a stream of hot light beer. He looks at Moony, concentrating and then recognizing.

'Hey, you should learn some Slayer.'

He laughs at his own joke, but Moony doesn't even hear him. The boy has shown him the way and he follows him down the drain with a sigh. *Le thrill est gone loin de moi.*

Coming through the underpass onto Riverside. Lorenzo kicking at the slush, Moony watching for dark shapes that might want to steal his empty wallet.

‘I should go home, gotta teach tomorrow.’

‘Fuck those little snot-nosed primary schoolers – at least have one drink. Lotta the old crowd’ll be around. Just like old times.’

Old times. Sun coming up, booze still flowing like Onaping Falls, bodies piled like some trench in World War Whatever.

‘Don’t think I could survive a night of old times.’

‘One drink, s’all I’m sayin. So where’s that fucker Lepine and the rest of your goons?’

‘Home with the families.’

‘Sellouts, eh?’

‘Where you should be, with your daughter.’

‘What daughter?’ And he laughs like being a bad parent is funny.

They stop at an old red-brick place – sagging fence, curling shingles. Moony looks at the dark windows. ‘You sure Fitzroy’s still doin it?’

‘Lights were never on. C’mon.’

They walk down the gravel laneway and push through the overgrown hedge into the backyard. Lorenzo bangs on the tin door off the back of the house and they wait in the cold. Green, black and yellow of the Jamaican flag on the porch roof waving in the night air.

‘Lo, maybe we should – ’

The tin door shrieks open and Moony slips in the slush and falls back on his ass. Some large woman peers down at them, deep voice booming out, ‘Who’s comin for dinner?’

‘Natty dreadlocks.’ Lorenzo pulling Moony up. ‘Fuck’s sake, Nora, scared the shit outta us.’

Nora holds the door open for them and then wanders off into the dark of the house, muttering. The only light is leaking up the basement steps and Moony can feel the rumble of bass beat through his feet.

A small crowd is gathered in the basement, dancing, sitting on sofas, yelling over the music coming out of the eight-foot speakers. Moony recognizes a few faces – the bartender from the Frood, couple of guys from other bands, that drunk McGowan who is always in on every party.

Lorenzo drags him up to the makeshift bar – planks of wood laid across some old barrels. Fitzroy, six feet of skinny black muscle, rag over one shoulder, flashes them a gold tooth. Moony leans in. 'Ginger beer.'

A cup of green liquid slides across. 'T'ree dolla.'

Moony digs a handful of change out of his pocket, the last of his cash. 'Good to see some things don't change.'

He leaves Lorenzo yakking at Fitzroy and wanders off sipping his ginger beer. First the heat of spice, then the acid burn of overproof rum. Over by the furnace, a cafeteria table is laid out with an assortment of bowls and hot plates brimming with colours and smells. Moony pats his stiff round gut and grabs a plate, starts loading up.

'You gotta try the okra,' says someone scooping a blob of green vegetables onto his plate. He turns to see the brunette from the bar. Younger this close. Her eyes. 'And the fried plantain – so good.' Her lips. 'Here – coco bread's my favourite.' Her hands.

He opens his mouth to say something but the best he can do is 'Thanks.'

'Enjoy,' she says, swirling off into some other part of the party.

He takes a bite of the soft bread, the bit where her fingers let go. Lorenzo wanders up, drinking from a Red Stripe in either hand. 'You're old enough to be her ancestor.'

Out on the back step, passing the bottle of rum between them, the only sound Lorenzo sighing periodically and shaking his head. At the end of the lawn, the creek rushes on, dark and silent. A few dozen sighs in, Lorenzo stands, drains the bottle and throws it on the ground.

'Well, this party's done.' Saying it like a royal decree, and then another sigh. 'Let's go – I got a coupla malts back at my place. We can grab a quick one before I work.'

'You're gonna work like this?'

'Yeah. I should be there already. But I'll just sneak in the back. Let's have that drink first.'

'Naw, I should be gettin back.'

'C'mon, man.' The guilt trip in full force. 'One for the road.'

'Go home, Lo.'

'Aw, you asshole – what'm I gonna do?' Standing there feeling sorry for himself and it just makes Moony want to smack him.

'What're you doin, lad?' The other man shrugging. 'You got a good kid there – y'know that?'

'Yeah.' But he's not thinking about Emilia at all. 'Her mother left me.'

'I know.'

'Left me with fuckin shit.'

'She left both of you, Lo.'

'Yeah.' But he doesn't get it. 'I'm just fucked up, y'know. I was at the station cleaning when they brought that body in today – y'know, the one on the news. That kinda shit fucks you up, y'know?'

Moony nods because that's all Lorenzo wants, another free pass, another chance to share his masterpiece of pain.

'I miss her.' A sigh. 'That bitch.'

Another sigh, like all the breath leaving him, and Lorenzo staggers off, crashing through the hedge and gone, singing off-key and fading down the street.

It's enough to make you sick, because people are what they are, no matter how many chances you give them. Nobody really changes. Nobody really knows who they are to begin with.

Maybe he'll talk to her tomorrow after class. Take her aside. Talk to the principal too. Those things can get messy, though. Lots of paperwork. Lots. Messy to get involved.

Moony picks up the bottle and puts it in the trash bin off the steps, then sits back down to watch the creek. Keeping his eyes on it like he's waiting for something that'll just never get there.

Then she's sitting there. He didn't hear her, the door, anything. One second she wasn't there beside him and then, *pop*, she just was. She's got a cigarette wedged in her lips (her lips) and she's searching the pockets of her jacket, hands (her hands) working the buttons, and finally turning to him with this pouty look in her eyes (her eyes). He pulls a pack of matches from his own pocket, picked up at some old gig.

'Thanks,' she says, taking them, and he wonders if matches can go bad like milk or human potential, but the first one goes up in a puff of flame and he catches a whiff of mint. She squints as she takes a long drag, throwing back her head for the exhale, passes him the cigarette. Him smoking for the first time in a decade.

'It true you gotta suffer to play the blues?' Her voice almost a whisper, but the words feel so loud out here.

'It helps.' He passes the cigarette back.

She holds the cigarette up to her face, staring down the mouth of the ember. 'If I could sing I'd sing the blues for weeks and weeks and forever.' She laughs but it's a flat dead sound. 'I got so much blue in me I'm an ocean.'

'Which one?'

'What?'

'Which ocean?'

'I dunno.' She laughs again, but this time it's not the most depressing sound in the world. 'Which one's the bluest?'

He shrugs. Her next to him, her leg touching his leg. She's not smoking anymore, and he's watching the cigarette in her hand burning down like some kind of fuse. He can smell the menthol and he can smell her hair and he's suddenly drunk, more drunk than he's ever been.

All it takes is for him to turn his head to the left, to lean, and his mouth is on her mouth. His lips on her lips. A burning inside him. A burning on him.

He pulls back, slapping the hole the cigarette made through his shirt, the burn on his skin. One look from her and he knows it was an accident. She didn't mean it, didn't mean any of it.

'Francie?'

They both turn at the sound of the new voice. Some boy standing just inside the hedge. In a T-shirt, shaking with cold or anger. Something – a camera on a strap around his neck. The girl doesn't move away from Moony, doesn't say anything, just looks at the boy. She flicks the cigarette away, only the white bone of filter left. Moony watches it bounce across the snow – a starter's pistol and then everyone's moving.

The girl taking off the denim jacket, rolling it carefully into a ball. Crunch of crust on the snow, the boy walking toward them. Moony swaying to his feet.

Bang – First of July flashbulb rocketship boy's fist in his mouth and Moony's suddenly looking at the stars and wondering how standing up can feel so much like lying down.

When he sits up, she's gone. The boy is looking down at Moony, holding the balled-up denim jacket.

'You creep.' Twisting the jacket in his hands, trying to squeeze some kind of warmth out of it. 'You sleazebag. You perv. The fuck's your problem?' This kid spitting in his face, Moony thinking, He's going to hit me again. But he doesn't. Not with his fists. Talking to him like *he's* the snot-nosed kid, the one who should know better. 'The fuck you think you are?' And he doesn't know what he thinks. 'Answer me.' But his mouth's full of everything but words. 'Fuckin nothin, that's what.' That's what. Then, like another fist in his mouth, 'Used to be her fuckin music teacher.' Then the boy's back through the hedge and Moony's alone.

Her taste in his mouth, her warmth, the warmth of blood in his mouth. Crawling down to the creek on hands and knees, sucking water, spitting, trying to get the taste from inside him. *Le thrill est gone, bébé, it's gone pour de bon.*

Then around the creek bend, something comes.

A black shape.

A log.

Not a log.

A body.

Floating toward him. Floating by him. Pirouetting in the middle of the creek, the head swinging back toward him before it floats on and on out of sight. On and on and on, the current sweeping it away. The face – that blank expression, like death had come slinking in.

He lets go. Rum and menthol and okra. He's puking his guts out, everything he's ever eaten. He's puking out his knees and toes, the soles of his feet, every part of his body coming up in a rush, puking himself inside out, retching the last bits of colour from his body, spilling out like a wet rainbow, leaving only blue, blue blue blue, the blue of the creek, the blue of the sky, the blue of Moony. *Il est disparu for good.*

A light goes on. A light on his face. A voice asking him if he's all right, sir. A voice asking him what his name is, sir.

Moony opens his mouth and the words are there, so many words. 'I'm a teacher. I teach music.'

15

Heck Gilchrist watches Slim walk away, watches him go with his shoulders all hunched up in that T-shirt like he's immune to the cold, thinks, I'll go when I can't see him anymore. Slim reaching the top of the park and heading off down the alley, Heck straining his neck until he's out of sight.

He watches the yellow car across the street, thinking, I'll just keep a lookout until Slim makes it to the Bin. I'll go when he makes the corner on Grey. Back to the warm house on Baker, Mom's blueberry pie in the fridge, Dad maybe up watching late-night TV in the rec room. The sheets, the pillows, the bed. I'll go when he makes the corner.

He hears a rustling in the bushes and wonders if all hobos are cannibals or just some.

There he is – a speck rounding the corner right across from him. He waves, but Slim doesn't look up, just pulls the door of the Bin, a belch of smoke coming out, and then he's gone.

He watches the door, thinking, I'll just wait a bit, make sure it's all going okay with Francie. Just in case he needs me.

But Slim never needs anything. He's been getting himself into shit as long as Heck has known him. Always with that cocky little smirk and a shrug, like the shit could never be deep enough. So you go along because he makes it look so cool.

He waits, watches, but Slim doesn't come out. He might be in there fighting with Francie, or what if Milly's in there, or what if he's waiting in his car for Slim to come out? What if he needs him – Slim never needing anything – anybody – but what if he does, just this once?

Well, what can he do anyway? Milly is a cold-blooded psycho, for sure. Heck knows somebody that seen him kick a baby carriage once. And if you buy weed from him, even if it's through Dunc, he wants names and addresses, so he can climb through your bedroom window if you ever rat on him. Milly won't think twice about slitting his throat if he gets in the way. Maybe even stop to lick the blood off his cold dead corpse.

This was Slim's shit to deal with, he dug the hole. Last summer, he let Slim talk him into having a party at his place when his parents were out of town, and when somebody tossed the couch through the picture window he said, *Last time, Slim, I let you drag me into your shit.*

And anyway, Slim told him to stay out of it.

So he should just go home. The door to the Bin's not opening. The Beetle's not moving. He's just sitting here, his ass going numb, watching with a busted watch in his hand, so he should just go. That watch – his best friend's most prized possession in the world, and that kind of trust's gotta be worth something. Worth something more than watching. More than watching being what Slim would do for him – no matter what anybody told him to do otherwise. Slim the first one diving headfirst into the shit right after him.

So he's not going home. Not anywhere close.

'Okay, thanks, Irene – I'm headin out.' Wrapping her scarf around her head like she's Grace Kelly and doing up her jacket. She shuts down the rest of the lights in the dining room and blows a kiss to Velma, still cleaning up in the kitchen.

She pushes out onto the empty street, a wet chill creeping into the air. She turns her key in the lock.

'Mrs. Novak?'

Martha jumps at the sound and turns to see that chubby boy – Slim's friend, the one who likes her cooking – running across the road. 'Hello, Hector. What're you doin out so late?'

'It's not.' He's out of breath when he gets to her, babbling between gasps. 'It's not my – my fault, Mrs. Novak, I told him but you know – know him, never listens and I wanted to go with him, but he told me to stay put, but he's in trouble – big trouble – like really big trouble and I didn't know what else to do so I come over here hoping – '

'What trouble – is it Slim?'

'Yeah – he – he – ' Hector doubles over and pukes on the side-walk. She pulls a tissue out of her purse and gives it to him, letting him wipe his mouth and steady himself. She takes a deep breath.

'Was it Gordon?' The goon. She'd call the cops on him.

'Who?'

'Did Gordon hurt him?' She'd kill him.

'What? No, he stole some body and then he dumped it in the crick and then we gone in there looking for it and we been shot at and we almost got in a car wreck and now he's gone lookin for Francie and Milly's lookin for him and I almost got eaten by cannibal hobos in the park – '

'Shut up.' She shakes him hard by the shoulders. 'Someone's tryin to hurt him?'

'Yeah.' Hector looking at her with tears in his eyes. 'Someone real bad.'

Her mind sliding back to that afternoon at Nibblers – that stringy fuck in the red plaid with the rubber boots. Asking about Slim. And when she told him where to go, that cold look in his eyes. This is her fault. She should've done something then.

'Where is he now?'

'The Nickel Bin.' Hector gets his hands on her shoulders too, almost like they're holding each other. 'And we can't go to the cops.'

'Okay.' Her mind spilling out all over the place, running through all the faces she could count on. A short list, none of them downtown except Lucy, who'd only get her more hysterical than she feels right now. Coming back to where it all started. 'Okay.'

She grabs Hector's arm and they start off down the street, him blubbering beside her.

'Where're we goin?'

'To get some help.'

He looks at her, salty stains on his cheeks. 'Jeepers, you look old with your scarf like that.'

'Shut up and wipe your face.'

They're up Larch to the brick face of the Coulson, Martha scanning the building and then yanking open a side door and holding it for Hector. Her head's splitting because she's out of cigarettes and she doesn't feel like dealing with any bullshit. 'You can come up, but you gotta keep quiet.'

He nods. They climb to the top floor, Hector panting, and then down the hall, holes in the plaster and the carpet stained with puke and maybe blood. She doesn't know what number it is, and then she recognizes the cowboy boots placed carefully next to the door at the very end. So, he got them back. She knocks and gives Hector a quick remember-what-I-told-you look.

The door swings open and he's standing there, shirt off – filling the doorway. When he sees her, he doesn't look embarrassed or try to cover up. He's not showing off either. That's just the way he is.

'Hey, Gordon.'

He nods at her, like her knocking at two o'clock in the morning isn't out of the ordinary. Standing there, his pale skin stippled with old scars. Some she remembers, some new ones too. He looks at Hector, taking him in – the kid's eyes bugging at the size of him.

'This's Hector – a friend … of my son's.' Hector shuffles his feet and mouths *Hey*, Gordon's dark eyes shifting back to her. His nose going black with the bruising. 'Look, I don't know how you got those boots back, and I don't care right now. I need your help.'

And he doesn't ask questions, just turns and heads into the apartment, leaving the door hanging open. Almost empty, but what is there – a few books, a knick-knack or two, the glass terrarium – is placed carefully. Painfully.

'Wowsers!' Hector has snuck into the apartment and is staring at something tacked to the wall. The only thing on any of the walls. A hockey card. The pin right through the player's heart.

'Wowsers!' he shouts again and turns to look at Gordon. 'Number thirteen, Gordon 'The Python' Uranium, defence, you had forty-three goals and sixty-one assists and 111 penalty minutes in '67–'68, your last season. That's like a team record. You were gonna get drafted, like maybe number three overall – over*all*! Wowsers, my dad would never believe it – he said you were the best. Why didn't you play in the NHL? Didn't you want to? My dad loves the Jets. You coulda played with Hawerchuk on the Jets – that woulda been rad. I mean, you're old, but you coulda played with him when he was a rookie. Why didn't you?'

But Gordon doesn't say anything. Doesn't even act like he's heard. He pulls on a stained grey sweater and grabs his jacket and out he goes, leaving Martha to shoo Hector out, still waiting for an answer.

They take turns babbling at him from each shoulder, Gordon measuring long strides so that maybe they'll run out of breath and shut the hell up. Something about her son, she says, something about a girl named Milly, he says. The temperature's rising all across the downtown, vapour coming up from the sewers, and there's that tight feeling to everything. Something about this, something about that – someone's gonna die tonight. That's the feeling he's getting. Like skating the blue line, waiting for an attack, but the puck just keeps cycling back and forth, your insides getting sicker and tighter with each pass. You know eventually it's all gonna play out.

They get up to the soot-smeared brick of the Nickel Bin, and he tries the door – locked, but there're some lights on yet. He bangs on the door, metal ringing.

There's some muffled cursing, more noises, and then the door bangs open, Foisey standing there looking tired and crabby. 'We're fuckin closed.' Then, noticing him, 'Gordo, what the fuck – you come to return the slippers?'

He looks at Martha, cuing her to start the talking thing again.

'We're looking for Slim.'

'Oh, hey, Martha, I didn't recognize you under that whole schoolmarm thing.'

Gordon takes a look over Foisey's shoulder, the bar dark and empty-looking.

'He in there?' Martha says.

'He was bout an hour ago. Looking for his girl, Francie. Figure they're all down at Fitzroy's now.'

'Roy who?' Martha says.

'The speakeasy – you know the one, Gordo.'

He nods, never been one for parties, but he helped Fitzroy put a new roof on a few years back. Fitz pouring ginger beer down his throat and Nora sending him home with enough salt fish and ackee to feed an army.

Then the kid with the mullet pipes up. 'What about Milly?'

Foisey swallows hard and Gordon can see him turn nervous all over again like he did that morning. 'I told that kid, stay off the fuckin streets tonight. Some people just got a death wish, eh, Gordo?' And with that, he bangs the door closed. The sound of a latch turning.

Martha pulls the scarf off, letting the curls out. 'Lead the way.'

Gordon heads for the underpass, where it all started last night. Twenty-four hours hanging off him like a lifetime. What a fuckin day. Overtime, and it just won't end.

They clear everybody out of the basement, no charges laid, thank *criss*, and by the time the officer's finished giving him the inquisition, Moony's sobered up enough to give a look of shame and guilt sufficiently convincing to keep him out of the back of the squad car.

'Neighbour called in, said there was a fight.' The lump of muscle fondling his notebook. 'Who'd you fight with?'

'My stomach.'

The officer gives him a don't-be-smart look. 'I should take you in for public intoxication.'

Moony shuffles his feet in what he hopes is an apologetic fashion. 'Just a bad night, s'all.'

The officer sighs. 'You live far from here?'

Moony shakes his head and points vaguely. 'Just up the way.'

'Well.' The officer is giving him a look – the anger already fading to pity, something Moony's much more familiar with. 'Just get yourself home pronto, okay?'

He nods quickly, wringing his hands like something out of a Dickens novel. Keeping the act going until the squad car's off down the street.

Fitzroy comes out onto his front porch, leans on the railing smoking a pipe.

'Really sorry, Fitz.'

The old black man shakes his head slow from side to side, rhythmically. 'Not cool, mon.'

'Just wait a few days and you can get it all started back up again – same as ever.' But even as he says it, they both know. The clouds peeling back slow and an overripe moon up there. Things weren't going to be the same.

Fitzroy keeps on shaking and walks back to the door. 'Not cool.'

Moony tromps off down Riverside. The snow around Fitzroy's all stampeded by the partygoers, but when he gets to the next corner, it's still fresh. He's stepping on his own footprints in reverse – him and Lorenzo. And two more sets in the gutter, going back this way. Small ones, the girl, and the larger ones, the boy trailing after.

Taught so many kids over the years, he doesn't remember these two. Should he remember them? He remembers them now – tonight – isn't that enough? And who should he be more thankful for – her for her lips or him for his fists. He remembers himself tonight, remembers all of himself and that's enough. Start fresh from that.

He looks up and sees three people coming toward him. A big guy out in front in a green work jacket. Walking with purpose. He thinks about crossing over but it's too late.

He keeps his head down, hands in pockets, and they're passing on by, a non-event, until someone grabs his sleeve.

'Scuse me.'

It's a woman – pretty. Bad perm, but pretty. Nice eyes. He knows her from somewhere but can't place it. All these faces too much for him tonight.

'We're looking for my son.'

For some reason this chokes him up, maybe because he's still half in the bag, because of everything that's happened tonight, or maybe it's the image he gets of a little kid out here walking around and he thinks about the little daughter Lo left at home. Emilia. Good kid. Deserves better. *Va chier* – don't they all.

'His name's Slim.' This from the third one – a kid, some teenager with a mullet. The big one is standing a little off, attention elsewhere. 'All he's wearing is a T-shirt, maybe a girl with him.'

'Sorry.' And he says it with such feeling they're already starting to turn away. 'No – I mean, sorry – I didn't know you meant them. Yeah, I saw em just down the street.'

'That way?'

'When?'

'They still there?'

He's getting a headache from looking back and forth. 'Are they in some kind of trouble?'

She touches his arm. 'Please, I need to find my son.'

Young to be the mother of that kid, he thinks, but that's a mother – the love coming out of her raw and desperate. Messy to get involved. But messy not to. Just one big mess any way you cut it. Might as well jump in the mud puddle as slop around it.

He drops his arm, her hand sliding off, and just starts walking, following the tracks leading down Riverside and round the bend. Looking behind to make sure they're all following him. *Tu sais que I'm free, free maintenant, bébé. Je suis free de votre charme.*

She feels him back there the whole time, but it's not until she makes the turn on Annie, and there's the water stretching out in front of her, that she turns around. Slim about ten feet back, that denim jacket too short in the stupid sleeves. That stupid Polaroid around his neck.

'Slim Slider, I want you to get the fuck away from me.'

And she turns around again and keeps on going, knowing that's only going to encourage him. As she's passing the old brick waterworks, the pumps coughing away, he finally jogs up beside her, keeping pace.

'You hear me?'

'Yeah.'

She moans in frustration and walks faster, but he keeps up. Hands in his pockets, kicking at the snow. 'What do you want?'

'I wanna talk.'

'I'm done talking, Slim. I'm just done.'

He jumps in front of her, walking backwards. 'I'm sorry.' He's trying to catch her eye, but she just keeps her focus on that black water. The moon swirling like cream across its surface.

'I said I'm sorry.'

And she hits him in the chest, hard. So hard he stumbles back, his mouth dropping open like some kind of puppet. It feels good.

She hits him again before he can shut that mouth and this time he falls back on his ass. She stands over him and he just looks up at her.

'What d'you want me to do?'

And for maybe the first time – him lying there – he looks anything but cool. 'Nothing – you can't do anything.' And she steps around him, keeps on going for the water, crossing that barren patch of snow and dead grass and climbing over the boulders lining the shore. Mist crawling across the lake toward them. She sits at the very edge, her legs dangling over the water and thinks, This is the end. Here I am at the very end of everything.

Slim staying on his back, trying to let it all sink in. Let the whole day sink in and all the fuckin ifs of it, him and all that weight just sink through the snow, the earth, and keep on sinking. But he's like Lee Marvin in a bare-knuckle fight, he has to get up because surrendering just isn't in him.

He goes and sits beside Francie on the ledge a few feet above the water. The mist closing in, blocking out the moon. He doesn't say anything for a few minutes because she hates when he breaks her concentration – he knows that. He counts to two hundred under his breath and then finally tries.

'I should've taken you to Toronto.'

She keeps on staring out at the lake. 'Yeah, you should've.'

'I wanna fix it.' He swallows back the lump cause now's not the time. 'I'd do anything to fix it.'

'You can't. It isn't broken, it just … isn't anything.'

'So this is it – we're over?'

'Maybe – yes … I dunno.' And she looks at him and there's no anger there. 'I feel like I don't even know you anymore. And me – you have no idea who I am.'

'Sure I do.' She's that same girl in the shack in the summer and he's the same boy beside her. 'Slim and Francie. Francie and Slim.' Together on all the places they carved their names.

'If I turned back now, I don't think you'd ever really take me back.' And she's changing as she says it, older and older, until he doesn't recognize her anymore. 'But I don't think you'll ever let me go either.'

She's so close he could grab her. Keep her here. And he thinks maybe that's what she wants, for him to topple her, convince her she's wrong. The reflection of the water is in her eyes. And he wants to jump off the rocks because at least then he'd be inside her – in that reflection. He wants it to be different. He just doesn't know which one of them is right.

Here we are, the shortest distance, and it isn't close enough.

And he loses his chance, her turning back to the water. And without really even thinking, he lifts the camera from his chest and takes her picture.

And the flash stays on her, elongating – causing her to glow like a moth flapping against a bulb, the light never-ending, until Francie turns, raising her hand to shade her eyes, looking past him.

He turns with her. Two perfectly round headlights back in the lot flooding them.

Slim drops the camera and stands to face whatever it is that's coming.

Francie hears the sound of a car door, and the silhouette of a man steps in front of the light. She gets up, but Slim turns back to her and touches her face, two fingers on her left cheek, soft and quick, and then gone. The calm in his eyes making her want to scream.

The kind of calm she saw in that trunk behind Wembley so long ago this morning. A calm that just goes on and on.

Elwy's crouched at the front of the canoe, peering into all that mist, clinging to the surface of the lake. He stopped paddling forever ago, too tired and hungry, but Emilia's still back there, grunting with every stroke. He whistles high and clear, using his sonar like a bat on Marty Stouffer's nature show, trying to bounce his whistle off anything, but the mist just gulps it up.

He thinks about the Doctor Snuggles sheets on his bed, his robot pyjamas with the feet, the mushroom lamp on his bedside table,

Mom's kiss on his forehead – all of it missing from tonight. All of it maybe missing from every night. But maybe it's them missing and not everything else, and nobody looking for them.

He turns to look at Emilia. Her head down, putting all of herself into each stroke. One, two, and then she just stops. 'Em?'

Her paddle slides over the edge of the canoe, into the water, spinning into behind them. The mist chomping down on it, pulling it from sight.

'Em?'

She looks up, her eyes all big and afraid, not like any way Elwy's seen her before. Emilia's never ever scared. 'El, we're gonna freeze out here.'

He can't stop the tears, cold on his cheek. 'No, Em.'

'We been out here for hours. Nobody knows where we are.'

'Maybe your dad will come get us.'

'He'd be happy if I didn't ever come home.'

'Em, stop it.'

'We'll never play Commodore again.'

'Emilia Cecilia!' Elwy saying it in complete big-trouble mode. He scrunches up his eyes and makes himself stop crying, so Emilia won't be scared.

Then he turns back to the bow, purses his lips and blows. He whistles as hard as he can, as hard as Emilia hit Doug Degault when he said Elwy's mom was going to be a bag lady. Because sometimes you have to be strong for your number one best friend. You have to love them the most when no one else will. He whistles a beam of air like Voltron's laser, punching a hole straight into the mist, pushing it back. And there – the dark line of the shore in the distance. A street light like the soft glow of his mushroom lamp, calling them home.

Elwy stops whistling and starts to paddle, splashing water everywhere. 'I'm gonna beat your top score in Pitfall.'

Martha knows her son, even from the top of the hill. She knows the pinch of his shoulders, the angle of his head, the shape of his legs. A stretched, elongated, warped version of her boy, that small warm thing waddling around the house, bumping into everything. Arms stretched out, waiting to be picked up.

She sees the girl too – the one he was going with – a little behind him. But there is somebody else down there with them. The red plaid jacket – the man from the restaurant, the one who made her skin crawl, standing in the headlights of a car. What did Hector call him – Milly? All three of them down in the circle of light and snow before the shore, something big and bad and final about to happen.

'Gordon,' and he hears Martha's voice cracking as she speaks his name, an animal sound he recognizes, and he's off running, pushed forward by the noise.

He's got them pegged – one, the girl – two, bad news – three, the kid. Martha's kid, the same kid who stole his boots. There's no time to weigh it all, decide what was worth what. It's just real clear which way this is going to go without him. And the loneliness of that is too much to bear. There's no choice. Only him, a bullet train heading toward a brick wall.

And hell, if there wasn't that queasy feeling again, like this had all played out already.

One two three strides, and he's going down the ice. Tie game, last chance. All on him.

Slim takes a few steps toward the light, the silhouette not moving. Nobody asks, *Where is my brother*. Nobody says, *I don't know*. Nobody says anything because this has moved so far past words.

Then he pulls the black handle of the switchblade from his pocket. He fingers the hasp and out snaps the blade, stinging in the headlights.

Then the silhouette of Jyrki Myllarinen moves, something swinging from the shoulder and coming to bear.

Then someone big steps into the light between him and Milly. He recognizes the green work jacket right away – the asshole he took the boots from.

Slim steps to the side, finding an angle where the light isn't in his eyes. The big asshole gives him a look over his shoulder, a nod like, *I got this one, kid.* The guy who kicked his ass standing in against the guy who wants to kill him.

Milly takes in this new arrival, still holding the rifle at the ready. His gaze flickers over to Slim, those cold grey eyes knocking the air out of him – marking him – and then he moves his attention back to the big asshole. Drops the rifle and rolls up his sleeves.

It's like the War to Settle the Score all over again, Hogan and Piper squaring off. Heck's just outside the light, spellbound. Like wrestling, only even more real.

Milly 'The Maniac' with his legs wide, his hands spread out at his sides. He's twitching all over, circling slowly back and forth.

Gordon 'The Python' just standing there. Straight and still.

Milly's lips curl, teeth flashing out, some kind of animal – the kind that'd keep chopped-up bits of his parents in a freezer. The kind that could tear you apart with teeth and nails.

Gordon balls up his hands, knuckles popping.

Milly working in closer, so light on his feet he's almost floating. Jumping in close, throwing a hand up near Gordon's face – the big man not even flinching. A feint on the other side – still nothing.

Milly dances back, his lips moving, muttering something under his breath, a hiss – louder. He brings up his hands, gesturing, calling Gordon on. 'C'mon.' His voice a high sharp sound. 'C'mon with it.' And he keeps saying it, 'C'mon with it,' each time his voice getting a little higher and little tighter until the veins in his neck are throbbing and his eyes are ready to pop.

And then he springs forward, smacking Gordon across the face with a left, then a right, then another left.

Gordon's head snapping back with each one but his feet stay planted.

Milly grabs him by the jacket with both hands and pulls him in, driving his forehead into Gordon's face – his legs wobbling and taking one step back. Milly knits his fingers together and before he can recover, he lays the Double Sledge on him. Gordon stumbles back, blood flinging across the snow.

'Gordon!' Mrs. Novak running forward, Mr. Bedard reining her in.

Milly slugs him in the stomach, doubling him over, and then kicks him in the face.

Gordon drops to his knees.

Milly backs up a step, lets him waver there and bleed a bit.

If this was wrestling – if this was really real – he'd shake it off now, work up a rage, start trembling all over. Get to his feet and rip that jacket open, tear his shirt right off with both hands. And then the comeback.

Martha watching it all happen. Wanting to step in, to do something, but she doesn't know what. Always with Slim, she knows anything she could do is wrong. She just wants to pull him away, but she can't leave Gordon. Can't look away. Not like that last game. Her sitting centre ice. Gordon and that boy going down, one of them not getting up. And all the shit that happened after. He didn't come around anymore and she didn't call. They were both thinking the same thing. *Monster*. And years later when she saw him again, it was as people who used to mean something but don't anymore. She's not lookin away this time. Monster, nutjob, hero, mother, whatever the fuck they are, she's gonna look right at them. See all of them.

Slim can see the big asshole is a red mess. A hard breeze away from toppling over. But he's not even looking at Milly, all coiled up and ready to put him out. He's looking past him at Slim.

Not asking for help, not wanting it. Looking at him with such a softness – sadness for what he's done or what he's got left to do.

And then Milly's there, right up in Slim's face, breathing hard. He reaches down and closes his hand around Slim's, the one with the knife in it. Gently prying his fingers back to take the blade.

So this is fuckin it.

But it's not. Instead those grey eyes just look at him for a second. Long enough for Slim to know that they're not the eyes of a madman.

'Where is my brother?' The words so quiet he's sure no one else heard. And it's not an accusation, it's a prayer. The kind that can kill.

But before it can be answered, Milly's being dragged back.

Moony doesn't know what to make of this. This big guy bear-hugging Jyrki, whose brother he taught piano. And something in that image jogs his memory and he finally recognizes the big guy – Gordon Uranium, that hockey player who turned some kid into a vegetable, years back. Was going to be something big but threw it all away. Turned into a mute. Got by on odd jobs around town, from people trying to live off the fumes of a legend.

Moony doesn't know what this fight is about or how this woman's, Martha's, son is involved. But there's a knife and a lot of blood and someone's gonna get fuckin hurt, that's for sure.

Then something grabs his attention past all the action – a shape moving out on the water, coming to shore.

The Brawl to End It All and they're tangled up, falling back onto the rocks by the water, Gordon underneath, slipping a forearm up under Milly's chin, the other one across his forehead – the Sleeper, his patented move. Both of them flopping around on the shore like a couple of dying fish. Then even the flopping slows.

Milly's eyes bulging out, strange noises coming out of him. The Python tightening the choke.

Heck looks around – nobody doing anything – just watching. A high sound, somebody whistling, and he thinks he's hearing things.

Then someone yells.

'Whoa!' is the only word Moony can think of, so he yells it again. 'Whoa!' Running past the two twisted men to pull the approaching canoe up on the shore – the bow scraping over the rocks, paint flying. Falling back with the effort.

Two little kids crouched in there shivering, one of them whistling away.

'Elwy? Emilia?'

Gordon's choking the life right out of him. He can feel it, like squeezing a sponge. Another ten, twenty seconds and this guy's dead. Like that body on the television, like every body. The body laid out on the ice. *Crash.* How you go from that much noise to silence, he'll never know. Nobody moves. Players on both sides, staring at him. The blood coming out like a red hole opening in the ice underneath the kid. They came running on with a stretcher. Breathing, still breathing. And it should be a relief. Except as they cart him off, Gordon looks up. The score tied. A red hole left behind. Nothing moving on. Still five seconds left on the clock. Five seconds of forever.

Five more seconds and he'll kill this guy. Just another body.

Almost twenty-four hours ago Francie's life was so simple.

Five minutes ago Slim was about to die.

Four more seconds and Gordon's gonna kill this guy.

Francie thinks about all the photos of her that Slim took. All these pieces of her like dead skin cells scattering in the wind now across the slag up near their shack. Thinking, They're all pieces of my past, none of them are me. Just moments.

All Slim needs to do is keep her in his sight. He wants to shout, I see you, Francie! If he doesn't see her, she disappears. She stops existing. She stops being Francie. The Francie he's known for three years, three months, three days.

Three more seconds. Gordon just needs to hold on.

You can only hold on to a photograph. You can't keep what's in it. Not really. It's where you are out of the picture that matters. All those models, in those magazines – they're trapped. Forever. Like Francie, trapped in this town.

Slim just wants to break free. Grab Francie's hand and say, I'll take you wherever you want to go. Whatever you want. Just us two.

Two more seconds. Does Gordon hate this man this much? Or himself? For what he's become, for what he can never be? Where does he find this much hate?

And it's not hate anymore. She doesn't hate this backward town. It's just nobody sees her here. In this big fuckin mess of blood and noise.

If he loses her now, he doesn't know who he'll be.

Everyone needs to be alone to be something.

One.

He can't lose her.

But she's lost.

Nothing.

The world comes swimming out of the black and all of a sudden Milly can breathe again, and all he can think is, I'm still here.

Everybody's moving and talking. That big fella off him. Milly rolls onto his stomach, coughing blood, and slowly sits up.

They're crowded around a couple of kids up on the shore. That punk Slim in the middle of it, but the big fella off to side looking at him all funny. Then he just turns his back, walks away from the crowd to the lake, the mist all around his feet.

Milly circles around and comes up behind him slow, and he knows the big fella knows he's there, has to, but still he just stands.

Why? You had me, why'd you let go?

The lake is going calm and even though he's panting, Gordon feels the cold right to his root. A few months after, he took a bus down south. He'd never been to the big city and it took him a while to find the hospital. He couldn't remember the name, he just told the cab driver *Hospital* and the guy laughed at him in some other language. All the hallways squeaked, reminding you with each step where the hell you were. When he finally got to the door, he almost turned around and left. The kid was there, somewhere in all those cords and tubes and beeping things. Paul Katie – looking the same as when he hit the ice. The blood cleaned off so you'd think he was alive.

And what do you do? Do you apologize? He got a penalty. Five minutes for charging. They lost the game. They told him later, he didn't even know. Nobody was pressing charges. *Dirty hit*, some said. *The kid was hotdogging, asking for it*, said others. *Just a bad fall.* He knew the truth. The truth was this kid was good as dead, only nobody was gonna let him be.

All he could think was pull the plug. If that was me, pull the fuckin plugs. Please. Don't let me go on and on. Kill me or let me do some good. Maybe even kill me to do some good.

Five minutes, five fuckin minutes. How do you measure that against years, years and years of minutes. How could that ever be enough?

All day he's known someone's gonna die. Since that news report. Not the kid. Martha's kid. He could be something. You never know. And Gordon wasn't a killer. He had all the kill sucked right out of him by those cords and tubes. But this guy, this Myllarinen, he was a killer. It made him think of Katie. The man at the pet store told him, *You should think about defanging it, rip the venom glands out.* But he didn't want to hurt her. Instead, he let her bite him. Once. Let her sink her fangs in deep and held her there so she'd know what she'd done. Suffered through the pain so they both would know it wasn't worth it. She lost her nerve after that.

Maybe you can save someone, or save yourself. After all.

There it is – the arm coming around his neck. Bringing him back to the lake. He feels the heat off it, and he can't remember the last time he's been this close to someone, this still. The breath behind his ear, the smell of sweat and earth through the sleeve, the fine blond hairs on the wrist as the arm comes back, leaving him already – don't go, don't leave me alone – and then he's warm, so warm, so so warm for the first time in so long.

Warm coming out of him all the way down his front. He lets it go. And that lake so calm at last.

The big fella just lets go, drops to his knees – Milly helping him down, taking his weight and dragging him back from the water. Laying him out there on the rocks. The mist tight about them, giving them some kind of strange privacy.

All that blood surging out of him. His mouth working a little like he's trying to say something. He reaches out and Milly gets ready to bat it away, to go for Slim, but the big fella just takes his hand. Holds it tight. Looks into his eyes like this is all okay.

And then the rest goes slow, every muscle giving up. One by one. No death rattle, no explosions – just here and then not anymore. The hand slipping loose to the ground.

Hell of an easy thing for both of them. And he wonders if it was like this for his parents and for Lemmy, if they got some peace and if it was a hell of an easy thing.

He runs his finger along the entire length of the dark line at the throat. Trying to find a single atom of warmth in all this. Anything he can recognize in this stranger. But it's already going cold.

Ei, ei, et minua. Not you.

He picks up the Pystykorva and looks over at Slim. Turned from the crowd, facing him. Shock, fear, hope, so much feeling coming out of the kid, like he's cracking right open. More feeling than Milly's ever known. A twitch of his finger, a squeeze, that's all it would take. To snuff out all that feeling.

His hand slides down the stock and he finds the notch Ukki carved. Just one little notch, one bullet, but it runs so deep. The butt of the rifle pressing against his belly, the notch sinking into him – a shaft right down into the pit inside. It's his notch now, too. Just a squeeze, one more notch. And down into that pit forever. A pit, like this town, this one place he's ever known, without feeling.

It shouldn't be this easy.

He gets up and walks away from the body, passing Slim, leaving it all behind, and when he reaches the trees, there's a scream back there, but nobody tries to stop him.

He heads for the car, wondering if he should stop to pack another suitcase and how many hours he can get in before dawn. Going gone.

Martha looks down at the face, surprised she's so calm about this. His skin gone smooth, moving back through the years. Too young. We were never that young.

Not a Gordon anymore. Not a Van. Not anything. Funny how a person can go and still leave so much behind. This thing to signify the absence of a person.

Fuck's sake, Martha, she can hear Lucy saying. *Told you so. Obsessed.*

She must be in shock to be taking this so well.

But she looks around their circle – nobody crying, no hysterics. And she almost expects to see all their faces reflecting the same thing, but nothing's that tidy. All the others staring down, each of them seeing this in their own way. A breeze picks up behind them, carrying the mist back out over the water, taking some of the cold with it.

'Do you think he's alonely?' It's the little boy whispering, looking up at Moony.

'No, Elwy.' He takes the boy's hand. 'I don't think he's lonely anymore. Do you?'

The boy doesn't answer, he whistles instead.

No, he's not the one who's got to be lonely.

'What're we gonna do with him?' Hector this time.

And the question just hangs there, a thread no one wants to pick up.

'We should probably call the police,' Moony finally says, and then when nobody argues, 'That's what we should do.'

'Maybe they're already on the way.' Hector again.

'Maybe.' Moony taking the little girl's hand too, looking at Martha. 'Does he have any family?'

'I don't think so. He lived alone.'

'Well, we should call the police.' But nobody moves.

'They'll take him home?' the little boy whispering.

'Yes, Elwy, they'll take care of him.'

'No they won't,' the little girl pipes up. 'They'll put him in a black bag and then they'll stick him in a box and then they'll stick him in the ground.'

All of them silenced by that same image, that same feeling of having no place to go. The only sound the water lapping slow over the rocks. The mist has cleared across the lake, into the trees, and the moon comes free again, lighting everything up.

'No.' The little girl breaks the silence. 'We're going to leave him right here. This is where he wants to be.'

And she says it with such determination that Martha thinks, Yeah, that's what he wants.

'And we should wash the blood off so he can be clean,' the boy whispers.

And just like that, people are moving. Somebody getting a tissue and wiping at the face, somebody unbuttoning the shirt, somebody going down to the rocks for water. That moon hanging low over all of them.

Martha steps back when it's done. His skin so pure and white. The colour leaking out of him into the ground, like he's already part of the landscape. And she thinks about the snow covering him up and the flowers growing up through the rocks, vines climbing over him, the earth pulling him down, holding him close. Gordon slowly becoming part of the city. Finally belonging.

'Does anyone have a smoke?' Martha asks.

Looking from face to face, nobody answering. Stopping on Slim – like always, drifting somewhere far away on his own. And suddenly all she wants is to hold him so close to her, and it breaks her heart to know this is the only way to push him away. Sometimes you got to leave things behind. Sometimes you come back, sometimes you don't. But she's got to let him go. She doesn't know who she means, Van or Slim, but she's not waiting anymore.

Maybe it's time she took her name back too.

Her son looking up at her, giving her the trace of a smile, the most she's seen in a while. Then he pulls something out of his pocket, a strip of paper, and looks around the group.

'Where's Francie?'

Wally's been lying in bed for hours when he finally kicks the duvet off and says, 'I can't sleep.' Like anyone gives a shit in the empty house. He puts on his jacket and boots and grabs his mitts – the thick ones – on his way out.

He feels like he's spent the day getting probed on some UFO. His ass sore from all the plastic chairs he'd been plopped in all day, poked and prodded by detectives and investigators who kept asking the same questions over and over. About how he had effed up so bad, reminding him it was probably because he wasn't a real police officer. Wasn't really anything, really. No real value.

He's found his way over to the park and is walking along the beach down near the end. He's just about to turn back for home when he spots something up there on the rocks. Getting closer, he sees it's an old red canoe – and something else.

A man laid out next to it. Naked, pale flesh in the moonlight. The throat open and so much colour there.

He's got to blink a few times before he's sure this isn't some fever dream and he's still thrashing around under that duvet on David Street.

Fish saying something about everything always turning up in Ramsey and dammit if he isn't right for once.

'How the hell did you get here?' Not like it's going to answer, but stranger things have happened today.

All he needs to do is go up to any one of these houses here and ring the bell. So sorry to have disturbed you, but I'm a police officer and this is police business. A call is made. It's not going to win him any medals, but it might go a long way in getting him reinstated. And maybe Fish was right, he should look at going all the way, trying to get on with the provincial force.

And then those detectives and investigators will have something new to poke and prod and ask a bunch of meaningless questions about. Find some small grain of life left to steal from even this. Value and loss and life and death and who can tell how it all tangles together. You just gotta let the whole ball of yarn go.

Wally lays him out in the canoe, the head facing the water. He gives it one good push, scraping loose from the rocks and sailing out, following that moon as it sinks into the lake. There's a sudden tug in his gut and without thinking he pulls off his mittens, the cold snatching at his hands. The ring comes off so easy, and just as easy he tosses it into the lake. Hardly any sound at all for such a weight.

Another hard winter ahead, but tonight you'd never know. A warm wind carrying the canoe away. It's the clearest night he's ever seen.

16

Normando drives the Warlock over gravel, coming to rest at the base, and eases off the ignition – the shadows and ridges of King George above him. He sits with the window rolled down, sipping at styrofoamed cold coffee, thinking about things went wrong.

Eating an ice cream with Pat, sitting on a bench, when the parade came rolling down Durham a few years back. They had floats and some high school marching band and a pretty blonde riding in a Cadillac, hair all curled, hand waving with a big lipsticked grin. Miss Nickel. Right behind her came an old horse-drawn wagon, loaded with coveralled miners, smeared with dust and dirt. It was supposed to be quaint, but the horses looked dragged out of a glue factory and most of the miners were drunk. Retired, of course – the real ones were underground. The parade wound all the way up Elm, cars following in a procession to the new big coin monument on the hill. They cut a ribbon on the thing, Miss Nickel smashed some expensive champagne on it and Normando finished his ice cream.

He sips the mud at the bottom of his coffee and rolls tongue over lips. Tiger tail. He thinks now about all the cheering and smiling and backpatting of that day. Hell, he pressed his own shirt and wore a tie – almost forgot about things lost underground. All that useless preening, speeches about safer this and better that, just before they brought the machines in.

Somebody should wipe King George right off there. Wipe him off and put up a picture of somebody else. Like Normando, for thirty-five years spent underground, for his cheap company ring and his cheap little pension, or Bill Aho who got his skull cracked by company men, or Pez who lost his leg in a cave-in, or Xavier who went batshit crazy, or Gully with his ringing ears, or Scagnetti who went blind, or Lee with the shakes – or anybody, even Ristimaki with his two black lungs and his broken nose. Normando laughs at this. Ristimaki with his big ugly nose on that big damn coin.

Anything would look better than that perfectly wavy hair, that little smirk, all that damned dignity. Anybody. The boy, smiling, in a miner's helmet. How about the teenager he was when he went down and came back up again dragged by his boots. Put him up there. Celebrate that – have a parade. Take pictures with him behind, looking down on all this with a little bit of honesty.

Normando's been whispering out the window and he catches himself. Been whispering a story up at that coin, seeing the boy's face up there. Whispering about how he counted two short that one time – those damn Italians, always off poking at things they shouldn't be. Those rocks – this big. They sure talked about that after. For a while anyway. But Normando stops whispering. King George isn't listening. No one is.

Normando's crushed the cup. He opens his hand to the sound of styrofoam groaning. He staggers out of the cab, around to the back, and lowers the tailgate. He grabs a duffel bag and limps up to the monument. Standing at the base, staring up thirty feet into the night sky. Kids come out here and crowbar pieces off – he doesn't know that but it's what he's heard. Taking some kind of souvenir or trophy, some little chunk of glory. He leans against one of the columns, stretching up, but he can't reach the coin. Damned big thing. Planted here on the hill like some kind of meat thermometer, sucking the juice right out of the houses, the mines, him. Even from those two teenagers who were up here just yesterday – right here in the shadow of this thing, so real and alive. So much more alive than him.

His town is dying. Something else taking its place. Something spreading out, like that thing spreading through his insides.

He thinks about the long ride home. He thinks about turning the knob on his front door, swinging open, and what's left inside. Waking Pat up to tell her. A few months, a year tops. And damn all this silence. This damn respect. Let's talk about the boy. The dead gotta be talked about. Things've gotta be real and remembered.

Those kids yesterday almost gave him hope. That's what makes him so sick. They have to leave like all the young ones do, or stay to have the life sucked out of them.

He turns to look back at the lights of the city meeting the lights of the stars, all of it burning in the last of the night like somebody set a slag field on fire. This is the town. The city. Home. A place gets in the veins. Or you're born with it already in there. And it can't be dug out like they do in the mines. Maybe it takes putting the boy, his boy, in the ground. Maybe it'll take Normando's blood, too, before this big crater – honeycombed with the dead and dying underground, the stunted trees, black rock and sick lakes above – before it all caves in for good.

But in the quiet up here, Normando can see the whole town shiver like a bellows. That smelter sputtering smoke like a deathbed cigarette. Staggering on. Making it to another morning. The city breathes them in, and it lets them out.

Maybe they'll come back. Once they're done with their adventures. The slag cooled. When they have no place left to go, the city will breathe them back in. They can build on top of the dead. And make some kind of life in this awful and beautiful damned mess. He won't be around to see it.

Normando turns back to the big coin. He thinks about Joel McCrea on horseback looking off into the great blue yonder.

'All I want is … '

He pulls the zipper on the duffel, all kinds of metal winking in the moon's light. He takes out a hacksaw, laying teeth against the column, and starts to cut this big damned thing down.

17

Francie's got a seat all to herself, her legs wedged up against the one in front. Headphones on and the Walkman blaring and Bernard singing to her, *But for these last few days leave me alone.* And right now there's no grey blue loneliness in it. There's no colour at all. It's like the road – a dark secret, but rolling forward, and her riding the wave.

She'll stop in at her sister's to clean up. Then she'll go to that Mexican place, she'll walk the lights of Yonge, she'll ride those elevators up the high-rises right into the clouds. She'll do it all. Maybe she'll never come back. Maybe she will.

The song fading and out the bus window she sees the first glow of dawn, all kinds of colour bubbling up and breaking over her. Everyone else drifting in sleep.

18

Slim takes the long way out of town, the road winding through the slag heaps rising over him on either side. The white disappearing across the tops, the first snow already melting.

As he breaks for the highway, he looks for the big coin over his left shoulder, to let him know he's on his way. He looks everywhere but he can't see the thing. Must've missed it.

Onto 69, heading south. Somewhere down the road he spots the red glow of lights, the tail of a bus. He latches on, letting this be his guide, not sure how to let go. Not sure how far you can go on a spare. How far before he turns back.

On the seat next to him, the photo of her asleep in their shack next to the photo of her in profile staring out at the lake. Then the strip he found in his pocket, from the photo booth. Four little squares of Francie. The first one so clear and then she gradually fades out to ghost white by the last frame. A history of distance.

He knows they're dying. All of them. He just doesn't know what to do.

Acknowledgements

This book began in a Fredericton winter and ended in a Sudbury attic. Earlier versions of some chapters appeared in these fine journals: *Riddle Fence*, *Grain* and *Freefall.*

The work on this manuscript could not have been completed without the support of the Ontario Arts Council (Northern Arts Grant).

Thank you and much love to my brother, Warren, who took me on a lifetime of adventures, and to my parents, Stephen and Sara, for letting us play.

Thank you to Mark Jarman, John K. Samson, Jeremy Whiston, Bob Simpson, Sylvie Gravelle and Cristina Greco for reading.

Thank you to many other people for sharing stories and conversations: The Great Normando (Norm Jaques), Dan Bedard, Francie Morgan, Lara Bradley and Kristina Donato (Sudbury Flaneurs), Miriam Cusson (for *L'homme invisible*), Marc Donato, Mario Greco, Sadie and Nala.

Thank you for the soundtrack of this book: New Order, Kevin Quain, Van Morrison, Tom Waits, Men Without Hats, Rick Wakeman, Snailhouse, Greg Brown and the Weakerthans.

Finally, I give my most heartfelt gratitude to my editor, Alana Wilcox, as well as Evan Munday, Stuart Ross and the other truly great folks at Coach House Books.

About the Author

Matthew Heiti holds an MA from the University of New Brunswick. His fiction has appeared in many periodicals and journals, his plays have been workshopped and produced across the country, and he's a Genie-nominated screenwriter. He lives in a big old house in Sudbury with a little grey terror named Aino.

Typeset in Aragon.

Printed at the old Coach House on bpNichol Lane in Toronto, Ontario, on Zephyr Antique Laid paper, which was manufactured, acid-free, in Saint-Jérôme, Quebec, from second-growth forests. This book was printed with vegetable-based ink on a 1965 Heidelberg KORD offset litho press. Its pages were folded on a Baumfolder, gathered by hand, bound on a Sulby Auto-Minabinda and trimmed on a Polar single-knife cutter.

Edited and designed by Alana Wilcox
Cover art and design by Evan Munday
Map by Evan Munday

Coach House Books
80 bpNichol Lane
Toronto ON M5S 3J4
Canada

416 979 2217
800 367 6360

mail@chbooks.com
www.chbooks.com